Don't Lose This, It's My Only Copy

Don't Lose This, It's My Only Copy and Other Stories

Greenfield Jones

INK
BRUSH
PRESS

This book is a work of fiction. Names, characters, places, and incidents are products of the author's imagination. Any resemblance to actual events or locales, or to persons living or dead, is purely coincidental.

ISBN 978-0-9839715-5-9
Library of Congress Control Number: 2012941016

Book design by Arwin Burkett
Manufactured in the United States of America

Ink Brush Press
Temple and Dallas, Texas

Acknowledgments

Several journals published individual stories that appear in this book:
    West Branch, "Go, Purple"
    Great River Review, "The Grief of Terry Magoo"
    The Louisville Review, "Why We Like snow at Christmas,"
    The Thornleigh Review, "ICU"

Everyone knows that in all walks of life Networking is what really makes things happen and thus I want to thank my own Network, though the only member of it is Jerry Bradley. If you're going to have only one, he's the one to have.

Other Fiction from Ink Brush Press includes

Laurie Champion, ed., *Texas Told'em*
Terry Dalrymple, *Fishing for Trouble*
Terry Dalrymple, ed., *Texas Soundtrack*
Andrew Geyer, *Dixie Fish*
Andrew Geyer, *Siren Songs from the Heart of Austin*
H. Palmer Hall, *Into the Thicket*
Dave Kuhne, *The Road to Roma*
Myra McLarey, *The Last Will and Testament of Rosetta Sugars Tramble*
Eric Muirhead, *Cab Tales*
Jim Sanderson, *Faded Love*
Jim Sanderson, *Dolph's Team*
Melvin Sterne, *Zara*

www.inkbrushpress.com

For Sue, who often wears the anchor cross—the symbol of Hope—I gave her, she being my anchor who keeps me steady, keeps me from drifting.

CONTENTS

Prologue

Winston Churchill wrote that "we build our buildings and then our buildings build us." That is, the spirit that they materialize shapes us; true, but of course it is the spirit of the times—the Zeitgeist—that tells us first off how we should build them. Those that transcend the times that created them, or especially well exemplify the times, are allowed, some-times, to stand. Then we can revisit them to re-experience the verities—or lies—that, for a time, animated us or our ancestors. Until something happens to make them seem dated, they seem modern. Like us.

Often, that which changes things is a war, destroying, as it does, old power structures, creating new ones. Some say even that such is when wars happen, when the old forms are so out of place that they have to be destroyed—if not otherwise, then by violence destroyed, though wars ironically are fought to preserve the status quo and nothing more surely ruins it. This happens among the victors as well as the defeated, so that in a decade or so one has trouble discerning which was which. (Similarly ironic is War's morally Equal Opposite, Revolution: these are fought to change the Status Quo and usually change only the names of those in charge.) Economic cataclysms can do this too, or natural ones, or technological changes, or mass migrations. War is the obvious one, though. Through all this, now and then there happens a work that seems to transcend its time—one that seems to be of the Heilegegeist of Art instead of the au courant Zeitgeist. These few we only stand before and look on with awe.

Prince Charles noted that the structures going up the nineteen-sixties exemplified nothing. They were faceless, had no spirit. He was right, spot-on.

Others note that dances do the same thing—exemplify their times—except of course they have to be resurrected with dancers, for who can tell the dancer from the dance? An undanced dance is no dance, and a still dancer is no dancer. Thus, approximately, wrote Yeats. He too was right.

Here follow, then, are stories found not in a trunk but in a bottom drawer, found by a superannuated professor of English at George F. Babbitt State College (it began as a Teachers College and soon would be granted University status, or at least the title thereof) who on retirement was ordered to clean out his stuff but who until then had somehow missed or else ignored this ms. The title page was gone, so if there once was one it is not known. The new one is supplied here. The name of the author was gone too, and the old prof said he suspected it was left by a predecessor in his office, probably one of the sort who went into academe because he couldn't think of any other way to support his writing habit. The fellow seems to have been one of those who was not much noticed while he was there and was gone for some time before anyone realized it. It was he (probably) who left the stories. They seem to capture the Zeitgeist of that time well enough. Surely it was a time of dance floor changes as startling as the Charleston must have been to Turkey Trotters, who then were dated by the Foxtrot et al. In the early Sixties otherwise perfectly normal young people began standing in proximity of each other and doing a sort of Petit Mal, sometimes a Grand Mal. All without bodily contact. How far away seemed the Waltz, the first Western dance in which the couples touched (except in peasant rounds and romps). And now those dances are gone. But the stories remain.

I'm not sure what they're about, other than being about a time of change.

A Beam of Light

There was a kitchen at the Retreat Camp but it operated irregularly even in the summer and rather than disturb Maggie and ask for special service he got some cheese and crackers from a dispenser and a half pint of milk that was no more than a week old. He hadn't been there in months and was glad of it: not since Summer Youth Camp closed down had he been there. He detested Youth Work but since he was himself some ways short of thirty the Powers That Been had named him for the work that season previous. It had given him credit for the required summer of pastoral work. But so would his present ministering to a small congregation.

He sat and listened to music from a record player in Maggie's room just off the kitchen. She had on some swing music from the thirties that he had heard often enough. In sitting he saw between ceiling and stairwell a nice pair of legs descending though he saw them only from the knees down. Whose thighs and torso rested on those soft sockets he couldn't tell—not even the age (since folk grow old from the top down) and he lowered his head to see higher. A black skirt shielded the nearer limb but the inside of the other showed firm above a gartered stocking. He was minded not to whistle and was glad he hadn't when the legs brought down the stairs the rest of Gloria Tallman: bishop's wife. Closest call since he and Holly (then fourteen now fifteen and still his parishioner) had gone canoeing at the Camp in August and he had about done something compromising when another counselor came around the bend to where they were beached.

He edged the crackers off the seat to explain his bent condition and picked them up and rose to acknowledge her. About forty or a little less or more and blonde-maned she waved him down: Having a mod Eucharist are we Buckley? She remembered names well and he had once credited her husband's episcopacy to this facility till someone told him Tallman was already enthroned when they'd married. Perhaps half her life ago but they had no children.

You could call it that yes. Care to receive? To his surprise she came before him on slightly bent knee and ship's-prowing her hands before him opened her mouth. He broke off a segment and dunked it partly: Take this cracker and milk he said and put it in her mouth. He didn't know the proper words of institution. Never had occasion to say them. He'd given her too much and she choked as her lips closed on and sucked his finger tips then withdrew and when she could speak through the crumbs apologized.

He said it was his fault: Never done it before. She flapped her hand to dismiss the entire matter and sat beside him. If that's all the lunch you're getting it serves me right for taking so much of it. Then she looked quickly at him and he saw her eyes weren't green or blue as a blonde's ought to be but were hazel and were mapping his face nervously: a radar scanning device making sure of a target. Why are you here she asked: The conference isn't until tomorrow.

Conference?

Death of God. You're not coming to it? When he shook his head she sat back smugly as if they shared a joke. He now recalled a notice and registration form received some weeks back but he'd done no more than file it. No I think I have their number.

She sat forward and put her hand on his arm and scanned again. Oh he said I think they're just Oedipals. She didn't respond but stayed locked on. Oh you know—trying to kill the Father.

She shook her head and said No good: Who's the Mother? Assuming they're the Sons.

Oh. He put in the last cracker with his left hand since she still held the right imprisoned: Well I suppose it's the Church. They want that to

2

go on you know.

Even without the Father.

Just so. It might also occur to them that the Church is their bread and butter.

She breathed deeply through her nose and relaxed her grip and collected her hands in her lap. I suppose that's plausible. The clergy I have known. Then she laughed a little: embarrassed. She was not to have opinions on such matters. But she did: The psychiatrist she said Who examines potential postulants for the diocese tells me most men who think they're called by God instead are called by their mothers.

He had heard only that most of them were Passive Dependents (like submariners) but it struck him as true. He wondered if all that blonde hair was hers and indeed if hazel eyes didn't preclude blonde hair at all. As if reading him she patted firmly at the soft bun at the back of her head—the hair either was real or firmly attached. She wondered whether a Passive Dependent would want to slay the Father—didn't they love Him?

They'd need the Church: but they don't like harshness. Anyway that's only the psychological side of it. The theological explanation is that they were all once Barthians and the neo-Orthodox don't believe in the Historical Church. They think the Church happens here and there when God calls it into being. And now and then it goes away. All those fellows were once followers of Karl Barth. She thanked him for the lecture—or was it a homily?—and said she supposed that she too now need not attend the Conference. Anyway she said it was her opinion that most people believed pretty much the same thing. Then she rose and beckoning him up too put her right hand in his left and raised them while placing on his right shoulder her left hand and began moving him to the tempo of Pennsylvania Six Five Oh Oh Oh. Then she slid her arm around his neck and rested her head on him. Then as quickly as she had begun she stopped and twirled and left.

He sat and watched her legs kicking up the stairs. It was nearly time for his appointment with the bishop and he too went up but the secretary told him Mrs. Tallman had beaten him to it. So he waited.

3

Mrs. Kirsch, the diocesan secretary, had her hair done in so perfect a representation of a beehive that one might have thought her a Mormon bent on advertising that organization's symbol of industriousness. He knew that Bishop Tallman would allow no such thing knowingly and besides that she wore a pectoral cross actually an inch or so larger than Tallman's and probably two pounds heavier. It rested even then between her wall-eyed and outrageous breasts: half-loaves of French bread but fatter. She was otherwise a firm though not obese woman and they looked like something Lachaise had done to a statue that was otherwise by someone else. The weight of the cross pressed down her cream jersey and they jiggled as she typed: crucified between two thieves.

Once she had censored a poem he had sent in to the diocesan paper: it had the word womb in it. The Christian Century later took it. Fr. Waller who had suggested his sending it said she was probably a virgin. But she's married and has two kids. Adopted said Waller. Two thieves indeed.

Your name uh is it Buckley Campbell or Campbell Buckley?

He said and she typed something. He waited for more requests but that seemed all she needed so he went back to looking out at the lake. The bishop had moved the diocesan offices to the failed diocesan retreat camp in order to offset the claim (indeed the fact) that what had once been offered as his inspired vision was in truth a failure. His moving there kept it open year round and drew to it a certain number of a certain sort of priests and also a few laity who were retired and for lack of something better to do played Church.

Those were the sort who would come to the Conference. He would not stay for it. Being lay vicar of a mission in a town of 1000 promised an uninteresting weekend but one had to draw the line somewhere although he had nothing else to do—not even grade papers for the comp classes at the business school some twenty-five miles distant. The classes were filled with people either like the diocesan secretary or else who were destined soon to become like her. And who were very desirous of it.

4

As topography in that flat land went the camp was pleasant: there was a lake (grey and choppy at the moment) and some pine trees among the rocks on the shore swayed as they stood bunched together like drunken Marines. He had been a sailor and from time to time when he forgot what it actually was like he wished he had stayed in: he would have almost ten years gone. He thought like that when he was unhappy with what he was doing at the moment. Quite by chance he once had seen in a service manual that the military must beware the misfit seeking a niche for himself. That's what it would have been for him. So was being an editor. So was teaching comp. So was the church. Since he was unmarried he did not have to let himself get trapped though it was clear even to himself that he was drifting.

A light went on by the secretary's left thief (the unrepentant one) and she said without looking up that Bishop Tallman would see him.

When he went in the bishop was leaning over something on his desk so there was time enough to look around at the motel-modern styling that obtained also in this room as in every other. TEMPORARY was what it said: We call places after our own names but know not who will inherit them. That was from one of the Psalms. Not bad. Still that wasn't quite it in that this place was built not to be inherited and indeed it was not inheritable: it would fall down in forty years or less. The only substantial element in the room was the desk of heavy oak. It was a good ten feet across. The rest was drywall painted a nauseating green and the floor was covered completely with a tacked-down carpeting in cardinal Red. The old diocesan headquarters in a mansion bequeathed after the neighborhood became unfashionable was walnut-paneled throughout and had orientals on the floors. That was where the bishop and his wife dwelt. Here the filing cabinets looked more in place and the cords leading from sockets to machines seemed less from another world.

Dognuts raised his head for a moment to acknowledge the presence of his postulant and he showed an extra inch or two of beard. The scarlet notch was just visible in the step in his collar and in six months that too would be covered and he would look Low Church. Tallman was

5

not Low Church nor High Church nor Latitudinarian either: he was just Church. Before his consecration he had taught Greek for ten years at a seminary and though his ancestral tongue was Hebrew his personality was Classicist. Most of the heretics Campbell's own Old Testament teacher had warned him these days were New Testament men but Tallman was simply a Greek scholar not a New Testament exegete or special scholar. Unlike one of his (New Testament) professors who had told the class that We *say* the Creed. He had added when questioned about the Virgin Birth by Dave Williams that Mary was a theological virgin. Dave said he had once dated a girl like that and the professor gave him a C for the term. Then the bishop finished what he was doing and signed something and stood up.

While seated the bishop looked massive but when upright his height increased so slightly that actually it seemed to decrease. That there was a deficiency about his legs was generally known and noised about but since he never spoke of it neither did any other dare.

Sit down Campbell. He waved toward a steel and synthetic chair in a corner but continued to look just in front of his desk which probably meant that the chair was to be moved forward. With that done the bishop lit a cigar and looking up sideways asked whether his postulant smoked. Not much he said. The bishop nodded and said he supposed Campbell had heard about the latter's old roommate from seminary a fellow named Chauncy. No he hadn't. Really? Another sidelong glance. Well said Dognuts circling his cigar tip with the match Seems he's been tossed out of seminary.

Flunked his Greek I suppose.

No Campbell not everyone has trouble with that: anyway they would let him continue toward an L Th as you know though such failure would of course preclude a B D: lamentable though it is they would let him continue.

The bishop exhaled three perfect circles which interposed.

Though you would not. He smiled as he said that.

Tallman looked sharply at him. Perhaps I would—if I thought him too lazy or stupid to manage it I'd let him go on for a Licentiate. But, if I

6

thought him only malingering, certainly I would require top perform-ance. Yes.

He rested on an extra long ash tray his cigar which was from a box labeled Churchills. But Chauncy's case is rather different from yours. Haven't seen any ghosts have you?

Oh yes he remembered Chauncy did have that trouble. He was bright but he stayed awake nights because he was afraid of the ghosts in their room and thus he had to sleep days and thus he missed many if not most of his classes. So he hadn't got better.

They asked him to leave on account of his being afraid of ghosts then?

More precisely Campbell it was the seeing of them: any one in his right mind would be afraid if he saw one don't you know? But so few of us see them.

Buckley decided not to mention the case of the Apostles. No that was in the flesh. Of a sort that could go through walls and also be touched. That would shake you up worse than your run-of-the-mill ghosts.

If you're thinking of the matter of the Apostles Campbell that was different. I expect that you appreciate that difference.

He nodded more curtly than he had intended.

And how is your work coming?

About the same number attend: on the average a couple of dozen or so for Sunday and then when it's Evensong there are ten or so. Mostly Youth.

Ah you get on with the youth do you Good. But I meant your Greek: you're resolved to enroll for the summer brush-up course? He inhaled mightily so that a bright orange glow appeared behind the half inch ash already formed but not dropped. His eyebrows rose like bushy starting gates and revealed amazingly Gentile blue eyes pointed at him. The brows remained raised waiting an answer.

I suppose so. If I can afford it. My work at the Business College is only just meeting expenses and as you know my Rockefeller was only for one year. He hated the thought of Greek again. Of learning to use a

7

tool he didn't want to use. It was a great vocabulary builder though. The theological studies he liked: the more philosophical the better. And he had discovered one error of translation or rather of transcription in the NT but that was caused by his fondness for poetry and not by fondness of Greek. Of course the bare knowledge that he had of the language had made the discovery possible. He had not told Tallman what it was. Nor anyone else. Maybe he had mentioned it to Gloria Tallman.

The eyebrows had dropped again and only hints of blue broke through now and then like an early Spring day hidden by dark and hairy low-lying clouds. You know of course why we require Greek?

Because of its exegetical value? He stared out at the lake rather than look at Tallman until a peal or thunder brought him sharply around as the bishop's hand hit hard and flat on the desk. But as a careful student and writer of English I know how much goes into becoming expert in a language and I don't think I am able to give years to that task.

Campbell that is an unmitigatedly stupid answer.

Perhaps I ought to go for an LTh sir.

Nonsense. If ever you expect to be priested in this diocese I shall expect you to pass Greek then do your exegesis in it and graduate in due fashion. He pushed back from his desk and Campbell got up.

Where are you going?

Well I thought the interview was concluded when you pushed back as if to rise.

I dropped an ash on my trousers. He began beating furiously at his crotch with one hand while holding the cigar delicately aloft with the other thus giving the impression of an aged but meticulous masturbator. He mumbled that he thought he'd got it then said he thought twenty-five was not a very good number to have out for Sunday Worship. It was nearer seventy-five whenever he paid a visit.

True sir out of a baptized 300. That stopped the bastard: even he got only a fourth of them. And I understand that before I came to Trinity it was ten when they were visited by Fr. Waller. Not that I'm an improvement over Waller—it's just that I do live there and so they can pretend I'm one of them. They've been slighted rather stiffly all along.

The bishop while relighting nodded. It was indeed true: the town was one where the craftsmen lived not the white collar people. They hadn't had a resident priest in fifty years though for their first hundred they had one.

If it were more than Morning Prayer perhaps it would go up.

The bishop looked up: it had been the wrong thing to say. Morning Prayer had been the rule in the parish the bishop had grown up in (his parents never converted but they sent him to naturalize him) and his mind had not moved on that point in half a century. It was irrelevant to one whose love was the Classics and he preferred they not change. Here was a sometimes seminarian who preferred change: that was bad. He had to retrieve himself. The bishop did it for him: Well you do get some of the youth out do you?

About ten at Evensong sir: five or six are Youth. It gives them something to do—there's not much going on in Eau Sale. He slept in the basement of the church and GI-showered in the sink there and ate his breakfast and lunch there with the aid of a small reefer provided along with a hot plate and a toaster. When the organist came by they had eggs and bacon. Otherwise it was cold cereal and toast but the sandwiches were too predictable since he made them. Dinner at the Business College was abominable but at least hot: put a little Drano on it and it was okay. What he didn't tell the bishop was that he took the kids to see movies they otherwise would miss since they were under seventeen or couldn't make the thirty mile trip. They paid their own admission but their parents let them go since they no doubt thought he was a healthy influence on them and also it got them out of the house. He made them go to Evensong first. And they had to listen to his interpretation of the films on the way back: they knew by heart his refrain that All Art Contains Propaganda. They were getting pretty good at spotting it. Although only one girl was a regular among the half-dozen and he would have to do something about her and do it right quick.

Why do you suppose Buckley that as many as seventy-five turn out for my episcopal visits when the liturgy used is the traditional one Is it perhaps for the sermon? His eyebrows were raised again: Tallman considered that his Word was commanding indeed and that any sensible person ought to attend. He did have interesting illustrations and he used parables well. These helped enhance his common sense remarks. We are free to make our choices but not free to choose the consequences of our choices: one of his favorites. It was true though.

Partly it's that yes sir: quite a few come for the sermons then some are relatives of whoever is being confirmed and then there are the curious. Also, you have status that commands some attendance. Hmm said the bishop and his eyebrows descended. Truth was mainly it was the curious who came out: man does not live bread alone but needs his circuses too. And if Tallman were stuffy enough to stick with rochet and only a black chimere still he put on a cope and miter when he processed. Circus indeed. Even so he liked Tallman: because he rather liked the nineteenth century and Tallman was of that time. Definitely fond of it yes. Sometimes Tallman would take his text from Teddy Roosevelt.

Well enough of this: to come to the point Campbell what I should like you to do is drive my wife to the Conference tomorrow. The Death of God Conference. She has decided she wants to go. He looked up from a fresh cigar he was prepping: You were planning on attending weren't you?

Uh actually I hadn't quite resolved the matter in my mind sir: that is I think I understand these fellows and I didn't know whether I should come. Then too I have to teach Monday evenings so if the conference starts Sunday afternoon it might be I couldn't get it all in.

It'll be over in the early afternoon Monday. Had to schedule the Conference around Sunday morning of course since so many clergy want to come. Most of the laymen seem able to stay over and take a holiday.

The laymen who would come would be the same sort who went to diocesan and national conventions generally: those who could afford to pay their own way and could afford days off without asking. It went a long way toward shaping the tenor of the church and insuring the proper outlook on things. He agreed to bring Mrs. Tallman. The bishop was driving their only car to a meeting in the next diocese and Gloria had elected to attend this one. As a matter of fact I have asked you to do this Campbell precisely because you do know what it's all about. Gloria is puzzled and I want you to talk with her. Again he agreed. Now go home and study your Greek.

The secretary looked up at him impassively which told him his status was nebulous: at the cardinal rectors she smiled and at those in disfavor (homosexuals say) she frowned. So he was neither here nor there. Well that was better than being there. Her beehive had grown a pencil or two in it like brambles. More of a hornet's nest because of that.

The drive home in the 1963 John F. Kennedy Memorial Chevy II was as usual made without any particular haste he being in no hurry to get to his basement and being still less interested in being invited out of it for bridge or whist or some such. He was miscast. Again.

The car he had named as he had because everything else had been similarly named. It ran well enough. But it wasn't quick like Kennedy: Judith Exner had said Sinatra was cruel, Kennedy was quick, and Giancana was kind. But it ran steadily under skies threatening snow with clouds only a hundred feet or so above the older pines and the average-heighted deciduous trees: they looked like dendrites carrying messages across some blank synapse or so he thought till he checked the word and found that dendron was Greek for tree and that killed it—no good calling a tree a tree.

Still he wanted a metaphor for the yearning to bridge the gap between visible and invisible and he was sorry he had almost had it then lost it. Anyway it would snow. That was one way to obliterate the distinction between here and there: snow did that even if only by disguising here. Yet it was preferable even so to the forlornness of being locked in here with the there outside your invisible cage and un-available. The heavens hung low for the ancients said Tallman every week or two. The only time that happened for moderns was when it snowed. He slowed for the blind corner that marked the boundary between the diocesan and other rural grounds and the greater and uglier world beyond: a semi passed and a car pulling a camper trailer—

unlikely for that time of year—and then he was able to thread into the pattern on a four lane road. Tomorrow was Stirrup Sunday and mayhap he would preach on the obliterating snow. But didn't.

The alternatives were all Pauline and since he had never understood Paul he used the Collect for a text. They seemed neither more nor less impressed than usual and there were twenty or so present. Holly-the-Devout was in her front-row pew and nicely done up in red velvet and lace and never took her moist brown eyes from him not even during prayers. While the others filed out Holly knelt till only she and Mrs. McIntyre were left and while the organist was bobbing her red cockscomb do while loudly going over the hymns for next week Holly came smiling up swinging her long brown hair softly from side to side. He took a hand in both of his and said for her to decide with the others what flick they'd see but he had to leave just then for a Death of God conference. Holly's clear (except for one blemish) face clouded as if this were a bereavement he'd suffered and she'd not heard of and then realized it wasn't that sort of thing and she settled into puzzlement. Looking back to see if Mrs. McIntyre was faced forward and thus away from them he turning gave Holly a quick peck on the cheek and turned her purring from him and out the door. Then he went back to the sacristry to unvest and noted the organist's mirror let her watch the congregation even as she played so she might have seen. But gave no notice if so.

The Conference was only for one night but his suitcase needed more stuff in it than that so he put in two pair of fresh underwear and two shirts a pair of shoes slacks and a sport coat then the shaving stuff into the side pockets. The way the satin lining was ruffled and tucked it looked rather like a coffin he was filling albeit it was strangely shaped for one. He called for Mrs. McIntyre to be sure to lock up on leaving and stepped lightly out into the fresh-fallen snow and breathed deeply liking the sharp needle pricks it gave his lungs. The trees all had white crotches and stripings along their limbs so that a bunch of them together looked like a photograph that was markedly out of focus with the lens needing at least one turn. He saw Holly as he neared the edge of town and tooted and waved and she on happy recognition waved back: a near-orphan she lived with an aunt. His thoughts on the way to Tallman's alternated between obscenities involving her and ones involving Gloria.

Though the city in which she lived was the better part of an hour from the village there was no great open space free from occasional dismounted trailers (usually in clusters of three or four) and signboards and thick-walled houses put close to the roadside in an earlier age when such was reasonable. A couple of these now were bars. And so it continued till the more densely clotted urban blight announced the city: shopping centers and all other sorts of places that could be driven into and then the new suburban cantonments that stood looking the more naked from the tallness and plenitude of telephone poles and the absence of trees beyond the height of a man. Even in the snow they were grim though the snow helped.

Then came the old section which contained the last century's millionaire row where the diocesan mansion was that Tallman and wife now inhabited. Theirs was a brownstone turreted monster between a Funeral Home fraternal twin to the one side and a working girls' hostel to the other with a Toddle House across the street. There was a severe incline up to the place and he had to brake sharply before making the turn which was a good thing since the bishop came down it that instant like a bat out of hell and without a glance this way or that and broke across the street and into the fast-paced traffic the while causing a few honks and some skids and swerves by others. Then he was gone into the pink and lavender of the late November day. Buckley would remember to turn on the headlights after he picked up Mrs. Bishop Tallman.

He pulled under what he knew was miscalled a porte-cochere although he knew not the right name and saw her waiting on the other side of the cut glass windows. He switched off the engine and went around and opened the trunk to put her bag in which he supposed her faceted face was beckoning him in to do. She was halfway down the hall when he got in and she turned not to show where the suitcase was but to welcome him farther in. He followed: he liked the heavy walnut

13

paneling and the worn orientals: discretely dark oils were hung with several prints. She was in tweeds. It all added up to a style to which he supposed she was long accustomed.

We have some time for some tea don't we? She spoke as if the world might swallow them if they hadn't. Or coffee? she added when he hesitated. They had about fifteen minutes to spare and he said they could take half an hour. She nodded and went off to a pantry and clattered around and called back to him to sit. Feeling vaguely like someone's dog he sat. Leather chair: the real thing not any of your imitation stuff. Probably the Old Man's. He pulled a hassock over (also leather) and putting his feet up reached absently toward a box that looked like it contained cigars. Then she came back and saw him said Oh go ahead go ahead. She disappeared again briskly and he did take and cut and light. He could not recall ever having been offered one by The Man himself nor did he think He offered them to anyone else. Ah privilege. If only there were a fire in the grate.

She returned with the silver service neatly ordered and laid with cakes and jam and he supposed tea. Having set it on a table in front of the couch she stood back and brushed her hands on her hips as if saying now what else.... And perhaps from feeling a lack of warmth on her buns she turned and declared what was needed was a fire. She smiled and asked would he do it. There was a coal scuttle and he shoveled some in then lit the gas jet beneath it and looked round to see whether he'd done it properly. Apparently he had since she was pouring him a cup to the right of her seat on the couch. He reached for the cigar and the ash tray but saw it had gone out so he left it and sat beside her. One lump or two Her brow was troubled.

None. And seeing there was lemon sliced before him he asked for that. He was pleased to have done it right. He looked at his watch. Seeing him do so she waved a demurrer with her right hand while holding the cup to her lips with her left: No need to worry Buckley it'll be perfectly all right if we come in after dinner. Food there is made of pasteboard as you know.

I would have said plastic.

14

She thought while aiming intently at a fox hunting scene over the fireplace: Nooo I really must hold out for pasteboard. I eat there much more than you do and I think pasteboard: yes. She set down her own cup and raised the silver service to give him more which he hardly needed. He saw that half the pictures were fox hunting prints: part of a set and one was of a bishop blessing the hounds. When he laughed at it and she asked why he pointed it out.

Does it seem cruel to you or only silly?

Oh not much of either one. I just wondered where is the bishop who blesses the fox.

Her shoulders shrugged rapidly and she had difficulty getting her cup back to its saucer and some of the tea went up the back way to her nose.

I didn't know it was that funny.

She cleared her throat and reminded him that he wasn't married to Bishop Tallman. Eating a cake he agreed but without the faintest as to what she meant. Light your cigar she said while gathering things together. That is if you're quite finished with tea.

He was finished and he did relight and sat again in the cathedra and she went off with the stuff. When she came back she studied him seriously until he could no longer pretend not to notice and he got his feet down and readied to rise to go.

No don't. She came around to his left side and lightly pushed him back taking the cigar from him and after examining it carefully put it in her own mouth drawing gently then thoughtfully blowing it out. And took yet one more puff then lowered her rump over his lap she sat down and blew the smoke in his face. He reacted reflexively for the cigar and she put one arm round his shoulders as he did so. She kissed him lightly and then ended his awkwardness by transferring the cigar to him to put down.

Excuse me she said Do excuse my forwardness. He shrugged with as much savoir-faire as he could manage and she said But though I don't at all mind your smoking you see I didn't want you to taste like a cigar so I smoked it too. Tracing one finger tip around the corners of his mouth she sat and regarded him as a cat might a mouse she had firmly in paw as he thought of Joseph and Potiphar's wife: whatever he did would be wrong. So he did nothing. She kissed him lightly then seriously and after she patted his cheek got up and asked whether he was ready. For what? Why to go to the Conference of course. They could leave the things: the maid would take care of them.

You mean there's a maid in the house Now?

She nodded. Keeps to herself no need to worry. She handed him her coat which was a soft thing she folded around her across her front once he'd put it over her shoulders. The label had it that it was from the best shop in the city. The way out toward the retreat center was in fact past that very store and also through the slums surrounding. They send seminarians down here he said. She had sat quietly and made no noises but was prim and withdrawn. She said nothing now. The idea is that they will learn by living amongst city rats: they're sent down for three days with no money and no identification and wearing old clothes. It's supposed to be enlightening.

And did you go? She was looking quietly out her window at the flops the wineries the erotic movies. He reached over and pushed down the button to lock her door.

I went on my own. When I was seventeen and hadn't any alternative. Or at the time so it seemed. In another city.

How did you get out of it?

Joined the Navy.

She moved more approximately to the center of the seat. They were getting out of the slums then and toward the factory district soon to yield to the neon tentacles that the city sent out into the darkening countryside. I gather she said that you did not wholly approve of the Program. Yet I know the bishop was very proud of it.

Of course she would know rather well what was going on in the diocese and maybe even instigated some of it. Mayhap he had damned her program. If so then so be it. I am informed that it is the custom he said In Christian countries for middle-class evangels to be sent from time to time to preach to those persons existing below a certain socio-

16

economic level: I suppose those who choose to live the derelict life come to accept this and endure it as part of the price one has to pay for being poor. From the corner of his eye he could not see that she had by any sign committed herself one way or another.

Usually when we're sent to them we go wearing ties or else in dog collars or carrying Bibles at the least: anything to let them know that we're not one of them.

But that's just it: this way you go as one of them! And they aren't sent to preach.

Indeed. It would have been romantic enough for me to have done it voluntarily at twenty-six had I not done it necessarily a decade earlier. The point that you are missing Mrs. Tallman is that many if not all of those who are derelicts are assuming the role because they prefer it: they have this tremendous need to be unloved.

You should have fit in beautifully. Then she waited awhile and said Anyway Jesus went. Or so I'm told.

To get away from the Pharisees he said And to have a drink.

Jesus said it was to save the Lost Sheep.

Jesus said: but the truth be known He did it to get away. The part about the Lost Sheep was a ruse which was in fact the only one the Pharisees would have understood.

I see.

They rode toward the Center in no hurry since they had already missed the pre-dinner session which wouldn't be much anyway and he enjoyed the lightly salting snow and the patterns it made in front of the headlights and the impossibility of focusing on it as it fell. And her scent was pleasing so he asked after it. Ma Griffe she said Meaning my scratch or mark as in what a cat makes.

Sounds like a Southerner talking about sadness. But it reminds me of Paris: I was there once at the embassy and for a short time at SHAPE. Smells evoke nostalgia. A cheap emotion that nostalgia. She looked at him for more. Because it says there is something significant in the past that was good and better than now. And there isn't. Wasn't.

Perhaps it tells you that you were once alive whereas now you are not. She placed her hand lightly on his leg.

That's the lie I meant: significance is not to be found in sentiment. In some escapade at 3 a.m.

Napoleon said once that 3 a.m. courage was rarest in the world. Ne c'est pas?

3 p.m. is rarer. He didn't elaborate and it took a minute for her to realize Who he was talking about. Really she said You have religion on the brain.

A rare thing in a Postulant?

She nodded most solemnly and said she had known quite a few. He wondered how: she perceived it and stiffened. Not as you think she said. Then as if overcoming a hurt said The French (you mentioned you were sometimes in Paris) the French look on romance as a metaphysical exploration: for us it only means I'm alive. The hurt returned and she looked away though keeping her hand delicately to his thigh the way a priest might touch the altar while blessing the congregation: a sort of anchorage.

I think it was the snow that reminded me of Paris. That and your perfume. He saw her shoulders heave briefly and with her allowing the non sequitur to pass was awaiting the rest. That is he said The perfume triggered it and the snow made it possible to make the leap in time: snow eliminates time and brings the eternal in. Sometimes anyway. She sniffed something like really and said she had heard Eskimos had several words for Snow but none for Time.

She turned from him and wiped her eyes with a handkerchief she ferreted from a suede and floppy in-good-taste purse. It took both hands to do this and she kept them in her lap when she was done. She asked him to turn on the inside light and without asking permission she shifted the rearview mirror to examine her face and to arrange minor repairs. They were getting close. Maybe she said The reason they have no word for Time is that it's night for six months and then day for six months. She replaced her gear and latched the top of the purse through a soft loop. Did you ever think of that Buckley Six months of eternity? She shook her head and moved to an appropriate place farther right of him and said Well I think I like your version better anyway. Perhaps you have a soul after all.

Then she wondered how anyone could possibly live in a town like Eau Sale. Was he not isolated intellectually? Well he said He enjoyed talking with Bishop Pike but now that there was snow probably he wouldn't see him again until Spring.

Pike?

Yeah: in the mud.

Mud?

Burrowed into it. Most frogs do it. You knew he planned on coming back didn't you?

She had heard of it but hadn't thought it would be as a frog.

Neither did he: expected to be an intellectual again but it didn't happen.

She played it straight and didn't giggle: how did he know for sure it was Pike? After all most frogs look rather alike. And somewhat like him. Like he did.

The voice. She agreed immediately. Then too he said There was the matter of the magenta rabat: how many frogs wore those? With the white dog collar and a pectoral cross although all one sees is the chain of course.

The gold chain convinced her. She thought it a pity indeed he couldn't be with them. Perhaps they could contact him with a Medium.

He said that such was not possible since it could be done only while the good bishop was in the spirit world and not now that he was back.

At least he was interested in theology she said absently: most clergy weren't. She'd seen a survey of clergy and spouses that showed less than one percent had deep concerns about such matters. Indeed most people who go to church don't like to bother about theology or religious discussions of any sort: that's why they join a church—to be done with that sort of thing. They don't want to talk about or investigate religions. Except for Unitarians of course who do very little else.

Then why are you going to the Dog conference?

Dog?

Death-of-God.

Oh she said I'm just going. And I wanted to see you. Up close. I've had my eye on you. And you on me: I know. As for rest of it it's blabber: no one can prove or disprove God or even describe Him. She patted her bun again.

He turned the bad corner and began the circle to the motel-like Retreat Center. Except for the lack of a neon sign all else was tailored to that end: a portico to drive under with a few shrubs put out with gravel around them to keep out the weeds. But it looked better under the snow and from a distance seemed to give off even a bit of warmth. He left her off by the entrance and parked and carried their bags in: he took hers to the bishop's offices where Dognuts had a bed and shower and sink and toilet and then he took his own to the room that had been allotted him. There were two beds: one with an opened suitcase on it plus some clothes—black ones so it was a priest and it meant he was considered on the clergy side of things.

When he got back down to the lobby he saw most of them coming out of the refectory which meant it would soon be cleared for the meeting itself. He went as unobtrusively as he could to the kitchen and asked Maggie if there was anything left. The cook nodded and moved to the old gas stove on which some pans yet simmered. Mag looked like a nineteenth century Know-Nothing cartoon of an Irish immigrant: completely pink except for small bright blue eyes and a fluff of white hair on her top and an inch-long pug nose set over a two inch upper lip but she spoke Yankee and her churchmanship was Very Low. Her cooking also was Yankee. He got a plate filled with iridescent peas and carrots a Salisbury steak glued with a brown gravy and one baseball of mashed potatoes that hit the plate with a flop.

So you've come to the autopsy of the Almighty too eh? She didn't call him by name: probably had too many names to remember. He shook his head: I'm not here voluntarily. Bishop Tallman told me to bring his wife here so she'd have a way up and back but he didn't say I had to go to the fool thing and I don't think I will.

Hearing him say so made one kind of light go out of her eyes and

20

another come in. Now instead of telling him to read the Bible she said they should read it. Her speech went but poorly with what was put before him and he considered asking the Lord to turn it into food until he recalled the pictures of the malnourished that the Christian Childrens' Fund sent and which led to his mission adopting one.

Then in came Gloria who asked only for coffee. Mag gave up her chair and took another. Then at just the worst time Gloria asked what error Buckley had found in Scripture. Mag's eyes got a different glint with that one.

Not an error in Scripture just one of translation. Possibly. Someone (probably a redactor) changed a word slightly from ΔΟΚΟΝ into ΔΟΚΟΙ : since the oldest texts we have are in all caps the error in transcription is easily understood—just leave off a down dip and upswing and you go from Beam of Light into Beam of Wood. So it now reads that if you see a mote in someone's eye you should first remove the beam of wood from your own.

Mag's eye beams were on him now. Gloria was interested.

It makes the Lord into a weak logician and worse a poor poet: just because someone else has a speck in his eye doesn't mean you have a plank in yours and also it's a very bad image. Since no one can get a two by four in his eye socket. Greek physics of the day had it that we saw not by light coming into the eye but by a beam of light coming out. It makes more sense that way.

Gloria nodded and Mag shifted the glare to her. After silence she said hmpff and busied herself about the refrigerator. Gloria looked different but he wasn't sure how: combed her hair differently or changed her clothes. Or maybe it was a washed face and fresh perfume. Her jaw line was firm and that made it hard to guess her age: like the Madonnas in pietàs she appeared younger than she ought to be. Then Mag turned and asked her the Question: I don't suppose you're one of those who believes that God is dead. Her tone was deferential.

Gloria raised her cup and sipped: No she said Not at all—He's just gone away for a bit that's all.

He wasn't sure she winked at him and Mag simply wasn't sure. So

21

she offered Mrs. Tallman some pie and without an answer withdrew a pan from the reefer and began slicing into it. A plate of cherry pie that looked like red Minié balls stuck on cardboard was offered which was refused out of concern for weight. So Mag said Here Mr. Smith you take it.

He demurred but a finger was pressed lightly to his wrist as Gloria said Oh Buckley you do need some meat on your ribs. I'll wait for you while you finish it.

I'll take it to the room with me. That won it and Mag got him a clean fork to take along which he sheathed in his breast pocket tines up.

They left together but split up at the hall. She would see him at the evening session and perhaps afterwards for a drink.

I didn't bring anything.

She dismissed it with a wave: We have a supply she said and went off in gliding steps toward the room where most were already gathered. In his room he found a disrobed Fr. Waller resting his length on the other bed and a bottle of bourbon on the stand: he didn't seem surprised to learn who his roommate was. It was arranged he said When I learned you got pushed into this too. You going to the talk on the New Morality?

You're not I guess: Judging by your lack of clothes. His Field Supervisor had on shorts and socks and no more. Word had it that when and if Tallman left the scene this would be his replacement. He was popular and remembered names and faces well.

No I'll leave that to you young fellows who need educating: for me it's irrelevant. I came to terms with it long ago and you should too. Listen: members of non-dogmatic denominations Sacralize their Secular values because there is no binding theological or scriptural standard. Some decades ago nice people decided that they wanted to use condoms and you know what? God agreed! He replenished his drink and settled back. Did he want dogma? Waller sounded bored with the whole thing and said to get used to it: most people believed pretty much the same thing. He raised his head only high enough to drain into it a caramel colored draft. An ice cube shifted suddenly and he got a slop of it in the face. Patiently he rose up a bit more so as to gain a better vantage then after drinking he set down the glass. The part that had spilled on him he rubbed onto his beard like an after shave then wiped his hands in his arm pits. But you are going aren't you? Waller continued to stare at the ceiling intently enough that Buckley began to do the same.

Yes he said to the overhead lamp I'll be going just as soon as I find something to do with this pie. Want it? Waller grimaced. So it was put in the toilet bowl. Maybe I won't go. But he straightened his tie and tucked his shirt then got his hands wet and ran them over his hair. I'm not sure.

When he came back out he found the priest had put on black trousers and was fitting on some loafers of the same color. When Waller leaned over his stomach fell in round pleats upon itself and his scalp showed pink and abundant through the red hair that from the front looked thick. He got up and puffed into a black shirt and asked for help with the collar.

Thought you weren't going.

Changed my mind: Gloria might be there (forgot you were driving her) and she might tell the bishop if I'm not. Hell of a reason but there it is. As for the conference I'll lay it on the line for you: forget the theological quiddities. We're nice people—just ask us. With the right values. You're one of us. So what if we confuse Zeitgeist with Heilegegeist: it doesn't matter because there's no other way to do it. Short of being dogmatic and you don't want that: you don't want to Secularize the Sacred do you? And stop trying to put strictures on God: be open. He put on a gray tweed coat then took it off and put on a black wool cardigan instead while taking care to fill the pockets with tobacco and pipe and apparatus appropriate thereto. Have to look the part he said. He didn't smile as he spoke. Just Love and Do What You will. He pulled the door shut behind himself.

He shook his head at the silliness: everyone always did what he wanted to. No strictures on God. Smith and Eddy believed in God. Gnostics believe in God. In Corinthians Paul told the Gnostics that one of them was even sleeping with his father's wife. No doubt that was what the fellow wanted to do. And the wife too of course.

He would go to see if Gloria still was in her room since if he went to the meeting and she was not there it would be awkward to sneak out of the hall but if she wasn't in the room it meant she would be in the hall and he had better go so as to be seen there. He went whistling down the corridor inappropriate as it seemed for a motel. There ought to have been a heated pool and sauna room. Then he sought out a soft drink dispenser to look for a Pepsi which the bishop preferred the place stock since the full name made an anagram for Episcopal. He couldn't recall if the Mormons had bought significant stock in Coke or Pepsi. Cold drinks were okay but not hot. Theirs was the ideal American deity a professor at seminary had told him since their deity started Perfect and had been Getting Better. Even so if they'd bought Pepsi it would be a good bet to acquire stock in for one's portfolio. If one had a portfolio.

Around the corner was the bishop's quarters and after a swallow or two more thither did he wend his way. The door was open a bit and he had already got inside before he heard them and they were coming his way.

Then dammit why did you ask him to come here afterwards for a drink? He's my roommate as if that isn't enough to put up with.

I suppose you asked for him?

Something tinkled and he imagined she had a drink in her hand. Quickly he looked for a place to go any place at all. The door he'd come in was too far behind him. He stepped into a closet and had just got behind a black wood cardigan when their voices passed. He moved slowly behind a capa nigra which pretty much blocked them and he was safe.

No I didn't ask for him I was assigned him. I suppose Mrs. Kirsch did it because I supervise his work at St. Adolf's.

I see.

Which means I can't come back here after the talk since he'll be there then and he'll notice I'm gone.

Maybe he'll think you've taken up with Mrs. Kirsch. Her voice stiffened against what must have been a severe look: Or would he probably assume you're drinking with the boys? You do that don't you? Drink with the boys. There was a slam like a glass coming down hard on a table.

It is now Gloria or never: I'm not coming back.

She laughed: If not tonight then never? Then I suppose it is never Mr. Waller.

There followed a slap and a gasp and then the door to the closet came open and a red-haired hand reached in and only just missing his nose got the sweater. There were stomps and a door slammed. He could wait till she was gone into the farther rooms and then slip out but maybe if she went out for air she would want her coat: it was in back of him. Then he heard humming and gathering up noises and as she quickly passed by he saw a flash of silver and he was safe: she would hardly go outside in her slip. Then he heard the door lock and she passed again. Could he unlock it quietly and get out No: she wasn't leaving. So he pushed the cape aside and stepped out.

Her back was to him and she had a drink in her hand and something was being held to her face: maybe ice to cool the spot where she'd been hit. When she turned he saw it was half a cookie. Or a whole cookie she was sucking on. Her eyes were wide but calm and she went on massaging the morsel with her lips something like a snake with half a mouse left sticking out. There was a red flush to her left cheek but otherwise there seemed little change.

Behold he said In the breaking of the bread I appear.

She smiled and the cookie came apart in her fingers: she put the bigger pieces in his mouth and held her palm open before him to lick up the crumbs. It was a cheesy sort of thing and it went well with the port wine she gave from her glass. Then she finished it. And stood there. She said nothing but only looked at him. He began to feel like Mouse No. 2.

I uh like your pantoufles. Huh? He pointed to her feet softly shod in slippers that were trimmed in fur (probably rabbit) which looked oversized because of the fluff and which went awkwardly with her slip anyway. Complacencies of the peignoir he thought but Wallace Stevens'

25

woman though perhaps wearing angora fronted mules surely had on more besides a slip. It would have ruined the whole poem.

Shall we sit down? She led him to a couch that must have come from the former establishment since it was of soft brown leather and was large and old. A throw of orange yellow and chocolate was at one end and she put it over her knees then extended a portion over him. Take off your shoes she said And tell me about yourself. And when was it you became interested in the Most High? She turned her torso toward him and rested her head on one arm folded back on the couch.

Well it wasn't from reading the Classics.

Unlike the bishop you mean. In that case tell me again of the error you found in translation in the Book.

Probably a redaction error.

She shook her head to clear it.

He went over it again about people seeing not by light coming into the eye but by a beam of light going out from it: he said he thought it lasted through Shakespeare. When lovers' eye beams twisted and pulled them helplessly together. Theologians have tin ears but poets don't. He hoped he had said tin rather than ten the way the dialect he grew up in would have had it. They want to get rid of the Valley of the Shadow of Death because it's not a literal translation just a better one. Better poetry.

She nodded. Then she said So you must be pretty good at Greek after all.

No I just used a lexicon to check the word meanings. My Greek isn't up to the bishop's standards.

Whose is? But we never discuss such things she said: He keeps them to himself and I am pleased that it is so. Her forearms unfolded and straightened along the back of the couch till a hand was able to send fingers into the hair above his nape. It felt good.

But as it happens (to return to your earlier question) I first became interested when as an undergraduate I had to read some Jonathan Edwards for a class in American philosophy. I'd seen no theology of any sort before that and I figured his God must be real because no one would make up a son of a bitch like that.

Her laugh said that she saw that they did agree after all and her hand gave a slight push of his head toward her mouth and he came very close to being swallowed whole but he kicked a bit and got free except for a paw or two that were caught and were perhaps even then being shriveled by the juices of her digestion. He tried to say something but couldn't and she gulped at him again and got more down and still more and then he disappeared into the dark behind the glaze over her softly open eyes. Give me chastity O Lord he prayed. But not yet. And so he became the second mouse and very quickly.

He left her warmly curled on the couch and covered with the throw and the lights turned down still more. He set the lock before closing the door so she wouldn't be disturbed. He checked in the dispenser mirror and decided he looked all right.

He got a chair in the back of the room peopled by maybe forty to include Waller who leaned in a corner pulling on his pipe and Mrs. Kirsch who knit one purled two. Maggie sat in the kitchen doorway looking not too furious. Conned perhaps. The speaker was as ass from a Methodist seminary not far off who explained by speaking literary: as Robert Frost said it's tennis with the net down but yak yak Robert Penn Warren said that's when you're really on your own. Yak yak: we were on our own. Modern Man found himself in the Free Verse Condition: those who needed structure to control chaos could do so but great opportunities for creativity abounded.

Buckley was about to ask about Creativity since if it meant ex nihilo who besides a deity could create. But then the meeting was over. He had missed most of it and something may have been said that would have painted him a fool so it was as well. He went back to the room and replaced what little he had taken out of his bag to go home and to escape Waller. He had made it to the foyer when he saw the priest step out of the conference room so he stood behind a plastic-looking planter until the way was clear. Actually the plant was real.

The John F Kennedy Memorial Chevy II was cold but he was glad to get in it. The snow was dry stuff that the wipers easily swept in two protractor arcs. It was not slippery at all so he could make good time. When he turned on the lights their yellow cones showed that it was still coming down. Then he decided not to make good time by following the hypotenuse back to the town but would make a right angle that would take him through the town. It was four lane and well cared for. On the radio he couldn't get the CBC and good uninterrupted music but found a C & W from a thousand miles away. His high school physics teacher had explained about skip zones. Sometimes Mr. Muller talked of how fine it was in the Navy in WW2 but with five kids he had to leave it and as the coach he also used naval strategy to explain football tactics though to Buckley football always seemed more Army. Basketball was Air Force and baseball was Navy. Which being a summer sport they did not play at his school though it was all he was any good at. Love Oh Love Oh Careless Love. Well C and W was better than Rock.

He had to admit that Waller had a good point about Liberals confusing Zeitgeist with Heilegegeist. Possibly there was a homily in that. He would file it for further use.

He stayed under a limit even a highway patrolman would have set and enjoyed the dark suggestions of pines on either side. The lake could not be seen. He stopped at a Four Way and began to proceed cautiously when a car with no lights on and only a few yards from him came at him on his own side of the road: he braked slid then turned into the slide and straightened flashed his bright lights and went around the other car while it apparently got over to the right side of the road and even turned on its lights. A fool was driving that. A fool or a drunk. Then the taillights behind him went out and he supposed the driver not only a fool but arrogant. Same thing. On a moonlit night you could do that but not in falling snow.

He turned then to the other sparse traffic and the hillbilly station till it began to come and go in surges and became more frustration than pleasure. In a half hour there would have been stuff in praise of fidelity then murderous revenge then adultery then individualism and whoopinholler religion. Whatever way the Will bent at that one time: the Violent Bore it Away.

He passed the old diocesan mansion looking good in pink and green granite especially as paired with the funeral parlor next door. He parked and went to the Toddle House two places down across the street and was happy to enter the light and warmth of huddled humanity. He enjoyed watching the cook crack eggs with one hand while ladling stuff with the other and taking orders the betimes. He was good at what he did and seemed to like it. He spoke in a dialect near to the one Buckley tried to shed. He would have lots of onions on his burger and a side of hash browns and coffee. Perhaps he would have a piece of pie afterwards.

Outside there was nothing much doing with the only color coming from the dignified neon of the funeral parlor sign. The diocesan sign was still in front of the other former mansion but it was baked enamel and couldn't be seen in the snow. Then a man's face appeared and their eyes met and the fellow came on in. Had he been out there long waiting for someone to turn around or to exit? Maybe Buckley had walked right past him when he came in: people told him he was absent-minded and he might have done so. If so he could make it up.

The man came down and without taking off his coat sat next to him and smiled cautiously. He gave the fellow the menu he had been using and nodded to the counter man that it was all right. The man said coffee and pie. Buckley said Get a waffle too and some bacon. The man shrugged and looked back at the menu. The counter man looked at Buckley and was told And a side of hash browns.

The man smiled and still looking at the menu nodded.

The order was dispatched and both ate when their food came and neither one bothered the other with talk. A fat woman cab driver read a newspaper at the far end and a soldier ate something in between them. Except for the rattle of the paper there wasn't much noise. He paid the checks and left a portion for a tip.

Then the man spoke: what was his line of work?

Clergy said Buckley.

The man sized him up: That so? He agreed with his rhetorical question and the man said he'd had some experience along that line

29

himself: Name's Lazarus.

Not The Lazarus?

The man looked around before nodding quickly. Buckley gave him a but how? look and the man waved to him to continue silence. Softly he said It happened this way: I died and after my sisters got on to Him about it He raised me. But He intended to do it anyway: there was this here tradition that you could be dead three days and not really gone so He waited four days till I began to stink to make sure there wasn't no doubt. He held up four fingers or rather three and a half since part of one was missing. Then things started happening.

What?

They got after Him for raising the dead. Namely me. Then He got so busy He forgot me. Raised me up and left me: here I am.

How old are you The woman cab driver turned a page and drank from her cup but paid no attention. The soldier had left.

Well I was forty-five then. You figure it out.

Couple of thou.

About that. He tapped his coffee for a refill and got it.

So what do you do with your time. Play golf? Not in this weather of course.

Naw. Used to. Made some good investments and some bad ones. Lost a pile on the Great War: thought for sure them Krauts'd win it. Got something going now though and when it comes in I'm fixed.

For life?

He smiled carefully: You kidding me son? Well I got to be going.

Wait! He caught the man's arm and settled him partially back down. Now the cabbie was watching. He fetched out a buck and put it in Lazarus' pocket: that sat him back down. Huh?

Well he said Tell me what it's like.

To be alive a couple of thousand years? Okay I guess if you don't weaken. And look out for the women.

No no no: I mean Over There. Lazarus looked blank. I mean Dead: what was it like When you were dead for four days.

Oh. He said nothing for a while then shook his head: Nothing much. Quiet I guess: tell the truth it's been so long I can't remember. I travel a lot: been to Mexico. Got to go now son: look out for that woman that's after you. Lazarus looked levelly at him when he said that then turned to go: Hasta la luego. Then he was gone.

The porcine cabbie got up and walked over to the door doing a strolling rumba. He left a quarter for Lazarus too and went back to the JFKMCII. The road south was clearer and he was abed by 2 a.m. All that he had to do the next day for the Business College was to think of something to say to his classes. Since nothing interested them anything would do.

Mrs. McIntyre the organist woke him at nine (only she and the warden had keys beside himself) and asked did he know the news. He did not. At seminary they had played that bit by asking if someone had heard the Good News. On receiving a negative you were supposed to say Christ Jesus is raised from the dead. It always brought a groan and immediate repetition to someone else. Mrs. Mac would not be playing that game.

Well here it is in the last edition of the paper just down from the city. It's on TV too. She looked around and noticed as for the first time that he had no set. He read the headlines: the paper inclined as was usual to the Left and said the President had a new plan for Viet Nam and then in the first paragraph doubted its viability. The snow got two columns and a picture since it was the first of the year and then down toward the bottom it announced that Episcopal Bishop Tallman had been killed in an auto accident caused by the poor road conditions.

He tightened his robe about him and put the paper on the table to read while he asked her if she wanted coffee. As was usual she then put the pot on and he sat down to read more fully. The story was filed late and they hadn't much and weren't sure of what they did have so there were gaps and they hedged a bit.

Mrs. Mac stuck her head in the reefer and got out the eggs and bacon and two pieces of bread for toast. He always had to ask her to coffee but once that was done she stayed and cooked breakfast for both of them. He bought the groceries and since she was on a limited

31

pension she saved a bit that way. She got little pay for being the organist.

I hear he was drunk she said clattering two plates on the hard little kitchen table. The plates were ordinary white with green stripes of the sort beaneries had and the silverware said U.S.N.

I doubt that. He smoked cigars a lot but I never saw him drink excessively. Indeed he'd not seen him take more than a sherry but saying it as he had spoken it made it sound as if he had been on more intimate terms with him than was in fact the case. Was he messed up?

A broken neck I hear.

His beard will take care of that.

She slid an egg to each plate and gave him three strips of bacon two to herself. Then she poured the coffee and set out the butter cream (real cream) sugar and jam. She made the jam herself and it was good stuff. All I'm wondering she said Is what poor Mrs. Tallman is going to do and how she's taking it and all.

I wonder too. He was getting his breath back till she said that and then he lost it again before saying Anyway she's rich: quite wealthy in her own right. And she'll get a decent pension.

Mrs. Mac lowered her eyes and looked off to one side no doubt considering the paucity of her own stipend and pension. She's not old she said She could remarry.

With her watery blue eyes she watched him while waiting to be told who he thought she might marry. Her fiery red hair he thought natural despite her age though she must have worked to sweep it up into the hatchet blade that made her look to be a feisty little hen.

He shrugged: Maybe she'll find a nice widower somewhere. With her wealth she probably has a circle of friends we've never heard of. Mrs. McIntyre thought maybe Fr. Dally over in Earlville might do since he was unmarried and about forty-five or fifty. He said that was the wrong ticket: not the marrying type. And most other priests already had wives. He said he didn't know: Maybe she'll go back West where she came from. Or maybe it's Europe.

Mrs. McIntyre was filing it all for though his information wasn't much still she was the local who would know the most and what she gleaned this morning would rank her high that afternoon when others heard and sought details. He began to make things up: harmless stuff and bits and pieces that would make for more pleasant tea and cakes in several houses that noon and after. Then he went for a sink bath and afterward called Fr. Waller but was told by one of his children that both he and Mrs. Waller had gone up to the city to the Home. That meant Funeral Home. So he went too.

The roads were clear the plow having done its work earlier. Apparently it hadn't really been needed just used because they were there for use. He went past the high school where it stood one block away from the highway and separated from it by the football field. Holly would be there even then warming the folding seat of an old fashioned desk and would have been there over two hours. A century earlier she would have been married by her age or almost. When was it Jonathan Edwards picked our Sarah Pierrepont? When she was thirteen? Didn't marry her till she was maybe seventeen but he had a decade on her even so. Aaron Burr was a grandson of theirs.

At the Funeral Home there were many cars and quite a few men dressed in clericals stood about. Some were going in and some coming out from having gone in: Where the vultures are gathered.... He went in and signed the book then advanced to the room: a few flowers were in evidence but either these would be held to a minimum by decree or else people had enough sense not to bother. He tried to recall if the paper had said anything about where those desiring to express sympathy could send their cash. Probably there wasn't time to get that information in. Then he was at the coffin which looked to be of the expensive wooden sort. No one was there to be greeted first except for Gloria off in a corner being controlled by Fr and Mrs Waller. So he looked.

Tallman who was dressed in the black and white rochet and chimere and exposed from top to foot looked because of his ridiculously short legs to be some sort of penguin. There were no marks visible except he seemed suddenly to have become very old and looked like one who had held on only by a marvel those many years. He couldn't

33

remember what age the old boy actually was. Then as he looked someone came up behind him and closed the lower half of the coffin so that only the large upper part of the man showed and then he looked as if he had been stuffed into a box too small. There came a slight sound behind him and Gloria passed: dressed in black she got her nerves together and came back and went up to the coffin and put something in. As soon as she had done it she turned sharply and ran into him and finding him a convenient enough sobbing post stayed there and cried for the better part of five minutes. He held her lightly and noticed again how soft she was. When Waller came up to pull her away she jerked back and stayed where she was though crying less. Over her shoulder he could see that it was the mane of her hair that she had put in with her husband: a long and thick honey-colored wave bound by a blue ribbon. What was left of her hair was short cropped at her neck and the rest remained no more than three inches long. She got a handkerchief out of his pocket and thanked him for it and went away with it though taking his arm as she did so thus making him her escort. As they retreated to the end of the room he saw one of the undertakers close the top portion of the coffin as well and then two priests began to spread a pall over it. It was a deep purple thing with a superimposed red cross that ran full length both ways.

What are they doing with Morris? She stopped short and would not look around.

Taking him to the Cathedral I suppose. Do you want to go there now?

She shook her head. Home? No she wanted to go for a ride.

A ride? Surely Gloria you must realize that's not possible now. There were no people coming up to her but several were watching from a distance. You have to be careful between now and the funeral and afterwards too for a little bit until people get used to it. He spoke softly but knew his voice carried well and was worried.

All right she said sniffing as if for the last time: I'll be the very model of decorum for a week after the funeral is over. She looked him steadily in the eyes: Then we'll leave. He couldn't think of anything to say so he nodded. He had to go teach his classes. She understood that: Leave me to the Wallers. She put on a forbearing smile and turned to them and he bowed slightly and left.

That night was Altar Guild and because of the news it was inflated by two Methodists three Baptists and an RC. He was able to tell them the bishop's neck wasn't broken but that he'd died instantly when the steering column crushed his chest: Drove his pectoral cross clear into him. He said Mrs. Tallman was doing well and the diocese would have a new leader in three months or less. And what a mess that would be: lots of clergy would of a sudden decide to visit the larger parishes and he would have a new boss. Waller would be in there fighting and indeed was doing so already. Ah well. He would drive as many to the funeral the next day as cared to attend. Several wanted to and a second car had to be arranged. That was good since it would keep him from Gloria afterwards. The bishop's car had run into the ditch just past the crossroads so it must been Tallman who was the headlight-less idiot on the wrong side of the road who had almost killed him. He would keep quiet about it. And he wouldn't have to do his Greek.

He wished Pike weren't burrowed under: he would like to ask him about Tallman's chances of coming back. And they could carry on the Women's Ordination issue which the frog favored and he doubted: If Jesus had wanted it wouldn't He have done it? Either He didn't know enough to ordain women or hadn't the courage. In either case if Jesus was wrong on that one then He was wrong about all of it. The frog held that Jesus had changed his mind on it and had done so a long time before. Buckley sighed: how strange the church must seem to Jesus. All of them.

There were noises in the chancel and he checked it: Holly was practicing the organ after taking it up two months earlier and was doing fairly well considering. She must have come with her aunt. She smiled when she saw him and made room for him next to her. He indicated that she was to continue and she did. How much longer had she to go in school? One more. He would be back in grad school by then.

You should be pretty good at this by then.

She kept her eyes on the music and said she had always wanted to marry a minister or a teacher or maybe a poet and she thought playing the organ could be useful. He wondered how that would help a poet. As for the others it seemed she wanted a father. Except for the poet bit: whatever else they were they were not fatherly. She read him and said she knew she wanted a father knew it quite well but after the briefest of pauses went on playing the organ. When he put his arm around her waist she purred a little. Then a voice called out that he was wanted on the phone. Holly stopped playing when he got up and looked as if she would wait for him to return to begin again.

It was Gloria and he was glad he'd taken it in the office since small as it was it was soundproof. She wanted to leave soon and wished to see him that night.

No that's not possible: I can't come up tonight and I'm not leaving with you.

There was silence then Why not? Her questions weren't reasonable and he tried to remember to listen for the music and not the words. But his answers and questions were rational: why him? What was so special about him in her life? That's what came from messing around: not so much Guilt as Complications. Little could be got through to her since they were on separate planes and in the end he said he would come up. He told the ladies he had to go back to the city and that he would be late returning and that Mrs. Mac should lock up. Holly was still waiting for him but began to play as soon as she saw him: Non nobis Domine. He kissed her cheek and she missed notes but went on. He told her too that he would be late and then left with the organ swelling warmly behind him as he did so.

The cold air was pleasant and there seemed to be far more stars visible than the two or three thousand he had learned in astronomy were available to the naked eye.

He parked in front of the Toddle House and found her hunched in a corner where she said she would be. Hadn't they missed her? They think I'm asleep in the house she said. He ordered coffee then changed it to chocolate. Then he had to sit and wait for it to cool. Lazarus wasn't anywhere around: he'd have liked to introduce them. She said nothing the while only played with her own cup. He thought they would go to the car but she told him to follow her into the back of the house. He asked whether he shouldn't move his car farther away but she had difficulty understanding and then said of course not. The bridges in her mind were burned.

You could be a teacher she told him once he'd got positioned in the leather chair. She understood that it was not a bad life: quiet and not stressful. When compared anyway to the Kingdom of Bang and Blab. And she had some money left her. He said she was just not used to having no man around but he thought she would get used to it.

She looked as if she had suddenly realized he was an idiot: I would have left Morris in any case. His death had nothing to do with it. It was the merest of coincidences.

He said it made no difference.

She started to speak then interrupted herself: Another woman Who is she? Younger Prettier Have you slept with her Well have you?

Yes he said I won't name her: she's younger yes but not prettier—different—and no I haven't. So far as I know still virginal. He was glad he hadn't said she was prettier.

She went to the window and pushed aside the curtain enough to look at the Funeral Home sign: You know I think your God may indeed be real—none other would make up a son of a bitch like you. She said it softly but it was final and when he picked up his coat and muffler she made no move to oppose him.

As he passed the table humidor he picked out a few cigars and pocketed them and then fingered out some more. With her back still to him she said We'll talk about it tomorrow.

When he said no she stiffened so he added Not until after the funeral. A week. At least.

She nodded without turning. But she was fumbling at something on her front. When she turned he saw it was blouse she had unbuttoned and that she was unfettered.

That had taken courage but appreciative as he was of it he shook his head and while saying At least a week he opened the door to the

37

cold.

If you leave you leave she said quickly: You'll have left you'll have left it all.

He paused then shook his head.

The Uninvited

Tommy had left his mess of a partially constructed model of a Focke-Wulf fighter on the table and had run to hide behind the doorway at the top of the stairs to surprise his mother when she came up them. The radio was playing a song sung by Leggy Pee, as his father had called her, about "You had plenty money back in twenty-two, / you let other women take it away from you, / now get out and get me some money too." His mother was moving slowly, but he could wait. Then in the moment between jumping out and making noise he realized it was not a good thing that he had done: she was carrying two fully loaded bags from the grocery, from which she would have had to have walked since they had no car. Walked in high heels since she had to wear them at her work. She was dead tired. When he jumped she only breathed heavily and took the last step, then slid into the Pullman kitchen to set down the bags. He had not done well by her.

That was two or three weeks earlier and they no longer lived in the garage apartment not big enough for a cat to turn around in, and he didn't miss it, though there had been some good times in it with his mother making a game of ordinary stuff like wrapping gifts in bright paper way ahead of time, inexpensive stuff bought with her Christmas Club money. She stored them under the bed they slept in, and often she would make fudge. He whipped it alternating with her but couldn't do it nearly so well. She looked for things to do during the week, went out on weekends, taught him to play solitaire to pass the time. The radio always was going. At bedtime she insisted he start off the night by spooning up next to her back, and he did.

His mother had not told him why they were staying a few days with a friend of hers, a nicely dressed woman moderately successful in commerce at a time when only a few were, and it was while he was in the tub at that friend's generous apartment that his mother came in to the bathroom, flipped down the lid on the toilet, sat on it, and lit a cigarette. It was a big bathroom and not a converted closet with a tin shower and always smelling of the gas used to heat it the way it was in their former place. The toilet itself in the garage apartment was at the foot of the stairs and it smelled of gas also, but of a fouler sort: it flushed, but only to an open tank beneath it. She took a couple of puffs more.

His mother smoked when she was nervous but that was pretty much always so he didn't anticipate anything unusual: since he was ten it was still all right for his mother to walk in on him unannounced. Or so she would have snapped if anyone had challenged her on it.

She crossed her long legs and stared at a corner over his head and took a deep drag. She was proud of her legs, joked often about her always having looked like a filly. Then, still not looking at him, said "If I marry Spud what will you do?" Much later he would realize he was being set up, but at the time all he could think of was what she would want him to answer: she had not asked whether he would like to move with her to the outer fringes of the Midwest, but rather she wanted to know what he would do. What did she want him to say? He liked Spud as he had liked all the soldiers his mother had dated since the outbreak of the War, their ranks varying from Spud's two stripes with a T beneath it to the silver leaf of a Lieutenant Colonel, who took him along with his mother to eat at nice open-air places in the country, the only places considered healthful during TB season. Spud didn't do that but played with him a little before he was sent downtown to his father's mother's apartment for the weekend; when he got back on Sunday nights Spud was not there. But more than once he had been invited to chin himself on his mother's friend's biceps, Spud's arm tautly cocked behind his head. It was no big reach since the man was shorter by two inches than Tommy's mother but then he had to pull himself up. He could do no more than three. Spud had a couple of ribbons and had been in long enough and overseas in combat for a good enough portion of that time that he had sufficient points to return to the States even though the Japanese had not yet surrendered. The military gave points based on how long you had been overseas, how much combat you had seen, and so on. Spud had been in Europe and North Africa and then Italy since early 1942 and could count to ten in Italian; he refused an infantry commission in order to use the points to get back to the States. The Colonel called him a coward but a month later Spud saw that same Colonel on the streets of Louisville. But Spud was still on active duty.

Then the Army decided it would teach him to drive a tank—something he had been doing for three years—in preparation for shipping him to the Pacific; he turned one over on a training run and was thus sent to a psychiatrist who then gave him a job as a two-finger typist. Soon he would be out. Years later, when Spud was an old man, German-made diesel cars were quite reliable and for a time very popular in the States; a neighbor had one and Spud hated it when the fellow started it up in the morning: it sounded to him like a tank and it took him back to where he did not want to go.

So what would he do "I guess I'd go live with my daddy."

Still not looking at any place other than the corner over his head his mother nodded sharply and took a couple of more puffs, gentler ones now. Then she got up off the lid, partially opened it and flipped the cigarette into it where it hissed gently and briefly.

He had not really thought before of going to live with his father and certainly his father never had thought of it. Later he would think of his parents simply as having Pioneered the New Morality, but not then: theirs was the only morality, and somehow he did not quite measure up. His mother was dismissing him; perhaps his father would find him more amenable to instruction.

He had seen his father only once since early June 1944 when he had been taken by him on a boat with some drinking/hunting/fishing buddies—blue collar men from the plants where he worked, he

41

preferring such—and some women from a riding stable where he went when in town. "Siss on you, Pister," he had said to one of them, an ash blonde who found his wit irresistible. She was the one who was with his father. They had gone back and forth from one shore to the other, three trips in all. He had not realized then that his father was steering the craft under fire onto Utah Beach and discharging his troops before going back to the ships for more. Having resigned his Guard commission ten years earlier when he had moved to another state and tried to start his own chemical business, he had lost his toehold in the military and was thereafter too valuable as a civilian consultant to the war effort to be just one more artillery officer.

Later Tommy would learn the consulting his father had done was on the Manhattan Project. That part was true: once when his Uncle Harry drove Big Tom to the airport when the government called, Harry had seen a Brigadier bumped from the manifest so that Tommy's father could board.

The other time he had seen him his father had taken him hunting though only one of them had a rifle. Tommy had erred badly by speaking when his father was sighting his .22 on a squirrel and thus spooking the squirrel and ruining the shot: actually his father had been sighting his BAR on Adolf Hitler on the occasion of one of the Führer's rare visits to the Western Front and the Captain's radio man had caused the war not to end right then and there. That was why the rifle butt slammed against Tommy's head a moment later: his father admired George S. Patton.

Big Tom had lettered in boxing (and football and track) while in engineering school and while working full time and getting a commission in the Guard. And married and divorced for the first time. Before he and his mother split just at the eve of the War Big Tom had taught Tommy the rudiments of boxing, which served him well since his mother moved often from one two-room apartment to another, always trying to get themselves in a good enough neighborhood for the schools to be okay. Those neighborhoods were then in slow decline though much later they became trendy with the houses being gaily painted and refurbished, many of them lined with bookcases; his mother skimmed an occasional book but that was it and she needed no bookcases. Her daughter by her first marriage lived with an Aunt and Uncle in a new suburb, then on the fringes of the city, and Jeanne went to a private school, at some sacrifice by her quasi-adoptive parents. Tommy did not envy her but only thought her lucky. Much later he would try to live with a family—his own—in a house similar to the one she had grown up in, one with, above all, a fireplace.

At every new school he went to there was always some snot who wanted to fight. Tommy stood lightly with his right foot back, leaned forward and jabbed at the face, jabbed at the face—the nose, the mouth, the eyes, his father said—one more lick and he'll quit, keep going for the face till he covers up there, then a hard right to the gut, then back to the face, the face. Tommy never lost. But he had few friends. Except at one school where a boy whose father had died early in the war took up with him for awhile, but eventually he too wanted to fight, pathetically couldn't, and, worse, his mother stood nearby telling him "Remembah youah boxing lessons, Olivah, remembah youah boxing lessons." Alas, Oliver remembered them not. And then Tommy had no friends at all. A teacher noticed him, though, commenting in class to his great embarrassment about how lovely his hands were. Every girl in the class pretended to want to see them during recess. But they were good for fighting.

His father had six professional fights after college before settling down to being an engineer. Once when instructing his son, Tommy had slipped inside and punched his father in the nuts, for which he was spanked. Nonetheless he smiled from time to time when he thought of it. That was in the Virginia foothills before the war, where dogwoods and Judas trees and rhododendrons were beautiful in the Spring and the snow did not turn black almost as soon as it fell; he had two dogs, the air was fresh and the James River pleasant except downstream from the plant where his father was manager.

It was in the refulgence of the Virginia summer when he was five years old that he had his first and only real philosophical inquiry, it having occurred to him that if he closed his eyes the world would go away: it all depended on him. Therefore he resisted so much as blinking until it had to be done and then he closed them. He still could hear the leaves overhead being lightly laved by the wind and he reasoned that if he could hear it then it was there even if he could not see it. Extrapolating, he further decided that the existence of it all did not depend on his hearing it or seeing it or anything else. With relief he realized he was not the center of the cosmos: it did not revolve around him. He did not consider his dismissal of Santa Claus the previous Christmas (how could he get around their little town in one night and never mind Lynchburg only twenty-five miles away with untold numbers of children!) as being of equal weight. He was through with philosophy.

They lived in that company-dominated town in a house and had a servant, who lived in an apartment over the garage. That was far behind him but seemed a magical place, though he knew the servant was not happy with her lot. She had studied a globe they had, turning and turning it. He realized later that she was trying to learn something. By then it was he and his mother who were living above a garage. The servant had followed them to Louisville in order to get out of rural Virginia.

Thus he found himself living with his grandmother when her former daughter-in-law went west to marry. His grandmother Bonny had a clean place on the fifth floor of a building near the center of the city where he could smell the distilleries, breweries, the yeast of the bread bakery and the sweet and sour of the saw mills; the Harvard Classics were on a shelf on her wall and though she could read French and spoke German she never corrected him when he read the one about the three musketeers and the fourth one, Dee-Art-a-Gan as he called him. She was too tired from her long day on her feet at the central post office. She did not approve of the way the world was going: the wars ruined it she said. He remembered that but did not understand it.

At night he could look at the hotel, bar and gas station signs that came on and made the streets look like flat Christmas trees strung with rows of white and variously colored lights. On her bedroom wall, which room she gave to him for sleeping, she taking the pull-down couch, were pictures of her husband and his ancestors, but none of her ancestors. His grandfather had made a great deal of money and had drunk it all before putting his service revolver to his chest. That much he learned later, and obliquely; with his widow his status was that of a deity. And though she went to church at most twice a year, she sang hymns sometimes at his bedtime. Then had a glass of wine. Her radio never played music.

In the locale were one or two city rats who lived in the carved up nearby mansions waiting to be torn down and one of them, a dusty girl, had sometimes sought him out when he was on the streets. That was back when he spent weekends with her, maybe in the second half of the second grade, to which he had been skipped. On his grandmother's building the girl chalked fuck on every brick she could reach, and she could reach lots of them. She had yellow hair and was very matter of fact, told him about her boyfriend called Super, who was a couple of years older than she and who screwed her up her butt while she sat on his lap reading comic books. Or so she said. Tommy erased the word from most of the bricks until he got tired on it and decided to wait for rain. When he went to live with his grandmother full-time the girl was long gone.

Then he got to go west himself for part of the summer to the town in the beautiful middle of nowhere shortly after his mother was married there and he had a room to himself in his stepfather's mother's house which now was theirs. There was a dog next door that had whelped a single puppy that he played with. The mother seemed jealous of his doing so though he played with her too. When the puppy got big enough for the mother to take it on walks she would go as far away from the area as she could and then run like hell for home. The first three times she did this the puppy found his way back and then after that he didn't. Probably someone took him in.

The house was cozy if small. The toilet was outside and baths were in a tub and once a week but who needed those when there was an

45

artesian-fed lake you could swim? In a year or so Spud dug a space for a septic tank—a very deep one because of the cold winters—and then there was an inside toilet and a shower. Those were from a Sears store in the nearest town big enough to have one—ten thousand (Plato's limit)—about thirty miles away.

There were bass in the lake too though he never caught one. And there was baseball, at which he got to be acceptable. He met some boys who wanted to play ball and most of them didn't seem to feel a need to fight. Actually there were those who in a larger collection of people who were more tightly packed would have been bad news. But as the town was one-tenth the maximum size Plato thought proper for a city, they had no real chance to clump together. So there were no really good or bad neighborhoods. Then it was over and time to go to the train in the town big enough to have a Sears and a station where trains stopped and to go back to the city and his grandmother. His mother would visit at Christmas for a few days and stay with her older sister and brother-in-law and daughter. He cried only for the first few miles and then settled down. The world did not revolve around him.

Rake Hell

He did not go to church in those days, even on Christmas, having been raised by parents who pioneered the New Morality, and though he was trying to live his life as differently as possible from the ways they lived theirs, it did not include church. But he was awake and showered, dressed and fed by the time three of his fellow Lieutenants burst in, one of them being his roommate in the apartment a somewhat overage-in-grade Captain rented out to cover his own bills. The Captain was a Mormon who had a girlfriend he wrote to often; he was saving his wages by putting them in a money market. He had been a Radar Operator in WW2 but was then designated as Duty Not Involving Flying. There was no longer a need for back-seaters in Black Widow fighters as there were no longer any of those aircraft around but it didn't bother the Captain since he was a natural-born paper shuffler. He was planning carefully for his retirement.

The Captain was not among the three who burst in. An Ivy Leaguer was and it was he who was most shocked by Tom's appearance: "My God, you're green! I've never seen anyone so green!" The Ivy Leaguer had boasted of taking an enlisted woman to a hotel shortly after arriving at their posting, at which all four had arrived simultaneously. He said again that he had never seen anyone so green.

Tom did not especially feel green, but it was just past winter out there on the fringe of the prairie and he accepted the fact that he was not well tanned. The other two asked if he felt all right, if he needed a picker-upper. He did not need one: they knew well that he seldom

47

drank and never to excess. His roommate only smiled and shook his head at the refusal of the picker-upper. His roommate had met a woman twice his age and was self-consciously enjoying the affair, though that woman was not with him that morning. Since he had been missing all night, that probably was where he had been. Tom had a girl back at the university who had accepted his fraternity pin the year before who then said that such amounted to being engaged to be engaged. He became comfortable with that. He had not lived in a family since his parents split and he looked forward to not being alone. The fraternity house was his longest domicile after he turned six years old. He was among the quiet members of a moderately raucous house. He noticed in his senior year that about-to-graduate women who had been on the wild side turned to him as a target of opportunity: they had to marry at graduation. Three of them sought him out before he found Jane who was not that sort. Or at least was not yet.

The three repeated their concern for his apparent ill health. What developed was that they had picked up four girls and since they were one short they had come to him to make up the number. The girls, who had been waiting just outside the door, then entered. They were from a private junior college for the not terribly bright daughters of area doctors and lawyers and other professionals who wanted their offspring looked after. When the crunch came to academe a decade or so later— when the public universities expanded and there were enough Baby Boomers with doctorates to teach the new tertiary academic classes— that college and most others like it disappeared, though some succeeded in becoming four year institutions. Tom had seen the college and noticed that a bust of Athena in the waiting room of the place had red circles on the aureolas of her nipples lipsticked on. When he asked about it he was told that it was a local tradition for the new girls to do it. It would be washed off soon, but had not yet been. The place tried for class, but didn't quite make it.

The third member of the group, a semi-religious Jew from Chicago, had accompanied him on that jaunt to that girl's college but had come away disappointed. Although he had bought a wedding ring for his girl back in Illinois—perfectly round, he said, since his religion said that signified the completeness of the marriage—he went out often and almost as often brought someone back with him. They weren't choice types, but the fellow didn't require such.

Then they all left together, crowded four in the back with Tom's girl sitting on his lap. She had sweet brown hair, was shortish and a little plump and smelled good, rather like certain lightly powdered Easter candies he remembered getting as a child before his parents separated. The candies were in soft colors of pink or green or yellow or lavender with a hard crust to them and a chewy white center. He had seen them sometimes since but had never bought any. Her name was Liddie, from Lydia.

One of the three girls managed to bring the talk around to her having fallen. But her colleagues in chorus said "Only once," and she agreed to that, looking to the men for understanding. The other three stared straight ahead so she turned to him. He smiled.

Soon they were at a roadhouse. The other six went in and by some understanding he and Liddie were left behind. She got off his lap but situated herself closely. He still could smell the Easter candy. She looked at him intently and then faced forward: "My older brother has a friend like you," she said. "He drinks a lot and gets into fights and chases just one woman after another. And he gets them. He gambles a lot, too. I think he supports himself that way. He's really intelligent."

"Do you consider living that way to be intelligent?"

"Well you must since it's what you do."

She smiled briefly and he noticed her eyes were hazel, which he liked.

"Who told you that?" She named the Ivy Leaguer. "And the others backed him up. They said they couldn't live that way."

Actually he had spent the night very pleasantly and contentedly reading a book about a woman who under hypnosis had discovered that she had lived in another body in Ireland in the previous century. Much of the data she spoke of could be corroborated, and was. Later, when he got deeper into Intelligence work he found out that this was not ultimately convincing: he had been posted to Poland late in his career and was sent a magazine he had ordered which arrived in two weeks, the same as everything else sent him. But it had only on it his name (misspelled), a partial address (the street listed did not exist and had the wrong number on it anyway, and Warszawa was not mentioned): only Polska was there. Yet it got to him in two weeks from mailing, delayed by the police needing to read everything that entered that Soviet-controlled Intellectuals' Paradise. If the Polish branch of the KGB could do that, how much could invisible agents of the Cosmic KGB do? Quite a lot. If Fallen Angels did indeed exist. The only bad part of the previous evening came when he called his girlfriend's number back at her sorority house and was told by an ignorant sister that Jane was out on a date. So he was alone again. He had felt gutted and did indeed have a couple of drinks before he could sleep. His roommate had not showed up at all.

"You aren't bothered by my behavior?"

She smiled wickedly and said she wasn't. In fact, two of the other girls had wanted to be his date: they had drawn straws and she had won. She wiggled her butt in emphatic conclusion and smiled again.

"Okay, then," he said, and put his left arm around her shoulders, putting his right one across her lap, or almost. She accepted that, laced him with her own arms and leaned forward to be kissed and was obliged.

Why We Like Snow at Christmas

It was while the outside professor—a psychologist—was asking why in his thesis collection of short stories he emphasized sex so much that Buckley first saw the Gulf Oil sign glowing like a premature moon through the seminar window. It was surely the same one he'd seen from his grandmother's apartment during the war: often there seemed to be two Gulf signs there when the moon was the right height and color. In the many months of his tour as an ROTC instructor at the University while he'd also done MA work he had not noticed it.

He said for one thing it was the leading metaphor of the day and he supposed also that it was because it was damned by their culture that he emphasized sex.

The psychologist thought it hardly an ignored topic.

Buckley agreed but said that it was too much in the head: his grandmother had denied it certainly and his father was confused by it (it was axiomatic wasn't it that alcoholics were sexually troubled?) and his own generation was active enough but they tended to feel they had to justify everything. He supposed it was the Puritan heritage and he might as well blame them for that since they were blamed for everything else as well. He did not mention his father's profession: Nietzsche and Jung and Ingmar Bergman all had that in common with him.

The psychologist nodded and the turn passed to the head of the department who asked whether he liked Justine.

Did he mean de Sade's or Durrell's? (That got him a point.)

Oh de Sade de Sade.

No said Buckley Not much.

Why not?

He guessed he just wasn't much of a Sadist. Anyway de Sade's char-acters are stick figures—one dimensional not even two dimensional, much less three. Like all pornography.

The head laughed and from there on out it was easy. He looked from time to time at the Gulf Oil moon and when it was over the sky was darkening and it had begun to snow. The head wondered what he planned to do next. Ask for a school that had a PhD program he said and get going on that. He would stay on active duty a while longer yes. And so it ended.

In his car the canvas was soon covered enough that he couldn't hear the flakes as they lit and he had to keep the wipers going to clear two baseball diamond arcs. Yet he did not drive away since he hadn't planned it that far: the pressure of the exam had precluded that. Of course he had to take the thesis to the binder so he did that. And on the way there he thought of Mrs. Mowen.

He wondered whether it was the snow that had done it or whether it was the Gulf Oil sign: probably the confluence of the two since the one led to the thought of his austere grandmother and really the other did too because of the snow-filled glass paperweight she kept. Mrs. Mowen had been his sixth grade teacher and his grandmother had been only too glad when she had taken an interest in him. Indeed Mrs. Mowen had taken an interest in any number of boys who were so to speak vul-nerable—spawn of legally or by war or death parents who were—well, only too glad to have the teacher take an interest in their at least temp-orarily semi-orphans. She made out with them. At least he supposed she made out with the others too. Two others who had been in her peculiar care said it was only up to a point though he wondered if that point had been defined by her limited requirements or their limited knowledge. The limit with him had been stretched he later realized to near non-existence.

Well he had knowledge now and he would by God call on her and find out.

The phone book allowed that she had not moved: it was the same one-storey bungalow she had shared her half of with her mother (secreted somewhere in a back room). He recalled the mother resting funereally and fully clothed on top of a bed seen through an open door at the back of a hall: at night after a meal of tasteless chicken a wad of mashed potatoes and bright green peas when it was make-out time that door had been shut. Nor did Mrs. Mowen's mother take her meals with them. He remembered her only as being there. Eighty perhaps so that meant her daughter was then forty-five or so. If so then she was nearing sixty now. He could not locate an age for her though: that he supposed was common enough for pupils and their teachers.

Whatever age she had been then she seemed now to be the same age: You haven't changed.

You have she said and opened the door for him. He saw that the door to the room at the back of the hall was open and that her mother was not there. Your mother died. She nodded and headed for a corner and sat there in a large pink and blue flowered chair or rather she sank into it: her own dress was grown over with delicate lemon and tangerine flowers that made her appear to be a confused garden out of which hung two plucked chicken legs that ended in sensible shoes. Arms to match. Useless hands and her face the same marshmallow softness he recalled that she had always had and capped with the same soft brown hair. Her lips were painted pinkly in a cupid's bow that said 1920s to him. He had forgotten that about her.

With the wallpaper's fist-sized blood-red roses bunched on it here and there and the rug's orchid pattern worked into it he began to feel surrounded: that was how it was when he visited her just after the war too. Nothing had changed: it was the same wallpaper the same rug. On her coffee table the same New Yorker covered with a winter scene in delicate pastels: unless things had changed it went unread. It was written apparently for aristocrats of soul and taste forced by chance to suffer the casserole life. She was the very essence of casserole. Except for her boys: and maybe there too.

She looked steadily at him like a returned ghost (one he had called back and not she him) but she said nothing as he familiarized himself. When he saw the paperweight she smiled: it was similar to his grand-mother's—a well-crafted thing from half a century before that swirled snow if you shook it and it would play a tune if you wound it and held it up to disengage the stop-pin.

Where tell we where has my highland laddie gone? That was the tune. The one Harry Lauder could never sing again after the Great War because his son died in it as a kiltie. He said that his grandmother had one similar and Mrs. Mowen nodded. She's dead said Mrs. Mowen not as a question but flatly as a modest admission of fact. It was his turn to nod. It came to him that of course she would have seen it in the obits.

By way of bringing things up to date he said you can see I stayed in the military. She acknowledged that and when she asked whether he liked it he said that it was all right: she recalled that his father had served. As a chaplain he said In World War Two. And after that she asked him He did Indian work in South Dakota. The blind leading the blind: a drunk minister at Rose Bud. She heard that he had married there a second time?

Oh yes she said she knew. An Indian wasn't it?

It was. She was. But he'd lost touch with her he said after his father died without issue from her and she had remarried. Perhaps she too now was dead. Mrs. Mowen nodded to accept that: So many she said Are gone into the world of light.

And did she believe in the World of Light?

No she said And neither did your grandmother.

He had not known that: he did know that once his grandfather (whom he'd never known) had died that though she kept about her the artifacts collected from life in a manse or two she seldom attended church again and when her son became an Episcopalian in college and then went into their clergy she was more upset at his choice of a career than the church he spent it in. It was while his father chaplained in the Navy that he had lived with her and had been Mrs. Mowen's little friend. His grandmother had kept a minimal Christmas and only brought out a few things kept from year to year and hung them about. She disapproved of dancing and seemed to think rather more were damned than the 80% Jean Cauvin privately opined. Man she held in fact to be so despicable that she couldn't see why any god would bother to come in: it was the traditional Calvinist disposition and could lead to Unitarianism. But not much to Fun: admire as he did those persons who could dance through life without thinking about it he never could do the same. Always he thought and asked Why.

Mrs. Mowen sat looking aside and giving off little sniffs and sighs as if ingesting a meal instead of news and it occurred to him in the waning light that just as it was too early for him to make his move it was almost time for dinner. He asked whether she had plans for that evening. She hadn't. Then would she join him? He was thinking of something like Chinese. To that offer while still staring at the wall she assented with another small sniff and a sigh.

While she went to the back of the duplex to get ready he looked about the place: a small case of books contained volumes no newer than two decades before and one copy of Tom Brown's School Days looked familiar to him. Perhaps he had read it from her shelf. And Pilgrim's Progress: curiously he did not find it dull. Nothing much else struck him. No pictures on the walls. Thank God: probably they would be of flowers. And the paperweight: he shook it and the snow rose and circled and floated around the dancing Highlander but no music came. He jiggled it saw that the pin was stuck although he thought that with the small blade of his knife he could fix it. No time to do so though since she was even then turning his way out of the bathroom with the toilet bowl slopping and swallowing hard behind her: even as it cleared its throat she was there. He helped her into her mantle and they went out into it.

The snow was thicker than when he had come in and she marveled at his ability to drive so easily in it. He explained his years of practice in northern climes and she relaxed a bit then tensed again as their way took them past a hilly park that had been allowed to remain in part at least in a natural state. She had taken him there sometimes on mild days. Perhaps she took all her boys there. To ease her seat he asked whether she remembered taking him there and she said she did. You got lost there once in fact.

He denied it: never had he been lost. Certainly not in so small a park. Yes she said he had indeed been lost there: exploring a cave or something.

It was a shallow cave. No one could possibly get lost in that small forest or that small cave: it had a low overhead and went back no more than a body's length or two and at that it turned only once. Young people used it for love making he said. She wondered how he knew. Spent condoms he said: Lots of them. She wondered if he knew about such things then. Sure he said. She sniffed again and sighed and said nothing more until they got to the restaurant.

He marveled on entering it at what bad taste the Chinese had with their decoration: the individual artifacts were some of them tacky and some of them not bad but taken as a whole nothing seemed to fit together at all. Perhaps it was something in their philosophy or theology. She said she surely didn't know: she was only a grade school teacher after all and things like that were too deep for her. He undertook to instruct her: Look at the walls and how their red is uncoordinated with the yellow of the linoleum floor (although a strong yellow would have matched up nicely) and they have brocaded lamps here with tassels on them but they have neon by the cashier's desk.

Maybe it was that way when they got it.

No he said The linoleum is new: they must have chosen it so. A strange aesthetic. Maybe they take things one-by-one and don't try to make sense of the whole.

Like a Chinese dinner she said and sniffed again. She picked up her menu and read it without glasses or seemed to although since such bills of fare were so similar she could fake it and get away with it easily enough. Her small hands took on color by contrast with the while menu and the even whiter table cloth stained though it was with old abuses of soy sauce. She told the Chinese girl she had decided on American food but before the waitress could write it down he overruled her and they got the dinner for two. He watched the retreating form of the girl and remarked that he had always admired the looks of Orientals—except their rumps which were too small: possibly because they tended to be short-legged as was true of most cold weather people. He supposed that conversely was why those of South-of-the-Sahara Africans wore such rounded ones (they being long-legged hot weather people).

She sniffed and said that he was indeed lost. He took his eyes from the small buns of the waitress and looked at Mrs. Mowen for clarification. When you were in the park she said In the cave: you were lost. So lost Buckley.

He knew not whether he hated more her incomplete comparisons or her inaccurate memory. He said only that he was not Lost. She indicated that she meant it metaphorically. He said he realized that point although he hadn't: Were perhaps all of her little boys lost? Or were they only vulnerable—left with their grandmothers and that sort of thing? She breathed in sharply and faced him levelly and said lost. She excused herself and went to the bathroom. When she got back the soup had been delivered and he was cooling his with his spoon. I waited for you he said The way one dog waits for another. She corrected him: You did wait and have only pretended not to.

By then he had in fact begun. The soup was topped with crisp green onion tops and was good and he said so. She agreed. Was she glad she'd gone Oriental then? She said only that the soup was good enough: the soup was the same she said at all Chinese restaurants. Okay: a funny thing about it then is that it's like Oriental girls or for that matter all Orientals—they all look alike. She gave him the look that Shocked Liberals reserve for such disappointing occasions.

What I wonder most about is how their authors handle the descriptions: she was a small girl with tan skin straight black hair and almond-shaped eyes. You know: that sort of thing. She listened and waited for more and when nothing more was coming she explained that actually each person was distinct and that he could tell differences if he wished.

She said here comes our girl now with our main courses. He looked and said no that was not their girl that she must be carrying stuff to

57

another table. And so she was. The Navy for a time he said Set me to sailing the Sea of Japan.

Ah so you can tell one from another.

Indeed. I notice you speak it.

She denied it and by the time he explained about ah so the joke was dead and their sweet and sour pork before them sat. Also some egg foo young. It also was good and he said so and again she agreed. The food he said had not changed. Changed? From the last time we were here he said. She did not recall having been there before. Really Mrs. Mowen you brought me here when my grandmother went to visit her son when he was in the naval hospital in Philadelphia and I stayed with you for a week: you don't remember that? She said she didn't. He said perhaps he recalled it since it was his first Chinese meal. Although as he also recalled she had ordered only a small Occidental portion. She didn't recall that either. But she did recall his grandmother's visit to Philadelphia: Your father had been injured.

Rolled I think is the word: rolled while he was drunk. Although of course I didn't know it at the time: she kept it away from me my grandmother did. Mrs. Mowen chewed slowly and sniffed and nodded: her mouth was working carefully over a morsel that didn't deserve the attention with her puckered lips looking like a sphincter. He would not have been surprised had they widened and excreted. Instead they stopped and she swallowed and nodded: Yes she said Your grandmother arranged it with the Superintendent of Instruction. Of course I recall that now: it was a pleasant week. She looked up then from her plate and from a brown puddle on it made viscous by too much corn starch: her pale eyes asked whether it had been pleasant for him. He reassured her and she returned to messing on her china. His grandmother had put her through it indeed when she checked out Mrs. Mowen for acceptability: told her of the glorious family history and the name of Buccleuch and their loyalty to Charlie and all and how well they'd done in the antebellum South and not poorly afterwards except for some temporary aberrations. She meant by that her son. In truth they were Scotch-Irishers and poor like the rest of the White Savages they were called and at best middling people on this side of the drink as well. But Mrs. Mowen accepted it all calmly or pretended to.

He turned seriously to his dinner and finished ahead of her. Silence began to scrape across their plates do seldom did they speak while feeding. He poured himself several refills of tea but she declined service: she only stared at him. He remembered that stare. Then came their fortune cookies with the check which he took. He opened and ate his cookie and palmed the fortune. She refused hers until he insisted and then she couldn't break it so he did. She crunched carefully at the offering and it occurred to him that possibly her teeth were false. He read aloud his fortune: O Snow the Beautiful Snow and Joy. He showed it to her and she remarked on the lack of punctuation. Is old Oriental custom he said: What does yours say? She looked and began holding it farther away till she ran out of arm. He glanced over and said Do Not Travel by Air. He laughed but she didn't: It's incongruous he said That mine should be so rhapsodic and yours so banal.

And so damning she said. He agreed that it was an odd thing to put in a cookie: was she planning a trip soon? Yes she said she was going to Florida the next week—to visit a young student of yours? She reached for her purse. Pretty well fixed he decided to vacation there over Christmas. She began to push back and he put out a tip and went around to assist. Once they were in the car he asked whether she wanted a movie: he owed her a full date he said since some time back she had paid for so many or theirs and as for himself he had nowhere in particular to go. She was uncertain as to what was on that was good but if he knew of anything then okay. He said they would drive past an Art Theatre he knew and see what their chances were and he turned toward the city to do so. The snow was clumping together thickly as it fell but as he swung up on to the particularly completed expressway suddenly they were out of it. And there before them clearly hung the Gulf Oil sign and alongside it a dull orange moon. Look he said It's like a Sun Dog or (to the erudite) a parhelion. She had never lived on the northern prairies and didn't know what that was.

It happens sometimes in the winter when the conditions are right: it has to be very cold and there need to be vapors rising. Then sometimes in the morning you'll see low on the horizon the sun and next to it its reflection shimmering there: it's caused by the rays bending a certain way and it doesn't last very long—only a few minutes at most. He said his father liked to use it as a metaphor for God the Father and God the Son and that his father thought the Indians liked it but with them one could not always or even often tell what they liked. Like a cheap movie Sioux Mrs. Mowen nodded and grunted. She appeared more interested in the innovation of limited access roadways that were beginning to reach out over the city even as was the piece of lattice they were on: she understood it was the President's idea to do it after he saw the Autobahn in Germany when he led his armies there during the war. Except in Europe they sent them around cities instead of through them: they did not allow that sort of destruction in Europe. He said he had not been to Europe and did not know. They left the expressway and descended again into the maelstrom.

The movie as it happened was a Japanese thing he had seen before as an undergraduate but wanted to see it again now that he was better prepared: it was basically a ghost story with all the ghosts lying about something that had happened centuries before: he remembered that much. Mrs. Mowen had not seen it so they went. It was a trendy place that had coffee and tea instead of cokes. Other odd couples were there as well and it seemed to him they fit right in.

Mrs. Mowen did not like the film: she preferred for things to be more verifiable than the Orientals made them out to be. He allowed that they were very precise on some matters. There was no point in discussing something they so differed on so he said nothing more on it and the only sound beyond the engine was the snow being packed beneath the wheels: when he came to a stop in front of her duplex it squeaked although it was not a dry snow. Looking at the consumed patternings of crystals going now this way now that (and both at once) he found them impossible to focus on: molecules that couldn't make up their Christogrammatic minds. A time he said Whose idea has come. She opened the door and got out.

60

When she found her keys he took them from her and preceded her into the short hallway. She seemed about to thank him for the evening when she saw he was almost out of his coat. He hung it and reached for hers which she only very slowly gave. Then he went quickly to the flowered chair and sat in it. That left her only the small couch and as soon as she had returned from the bathroom and seated herself he joined her there and put his arm along the back of it and behind her head. She leaned forward to get up and he reached after her and pulled her back.

Do you remember he asked, Some years ago when after we (you and I) had gone out somewhere together that after it was over that there followed a session on this couch? She looked determinedly straight ahead and said she had to go to the bathroom and he reminded her that she had just been. She stiffened but not so much that he couldn't turn her face toward him: he had never kissed a dish of mashed potatoes but the thought of it came as his lips left hers. Well yes he had done so—years before with her. Her breast was of the same consistency but he kept at it. Of old she had required that and just as then her eyes were shut and she trembled.

That could mean more than one thing so he worked further. Her flesh was all of it mashed potatoes but her breathing was coming shorter. Then he saw her eyes were not only closed but clinched. Still working with one arm and hand and still holding with the other hand he drew his face far enough back to focus and asked whether she didn't like them north of puberty. She said nothing even when he pulled her head back by her hair but she gasped sharply when the other hand pushed aside her teddies. He reached under her and learned she was not damp. Dry moss.

Then you really don't like them north of puberty.

Her eyes softened but remained shut: I can't help it she said I'm sick.

Sick?

She answered him not at all and as he began to knead her hair it made a crisping sound. Why not Bad instead of Sick He went on

61

crisping. You're chafing me she said at last. When he stopped she tentatively opened her eyes. Remove your hand she said and he let her head go. No she said The other one. He said he wouldn't.

No he said What you mean by Sick is that you didn't get enough ice cream when you were six years old? And therefore you can't help yourself? Well I can't either: you see I had this sixth grade teacher who corrupted me. So I can't be blamed for whatever I do: had you realized that axe cuts two ways? I'm sick Mrs. Mowen.

You were lost Buckley so lost. And I wanted to help you. That's why I took you in when your grandmother went to Philadelphia.

Not a bit of it he said and jammed his social finger into her. Her eyes closed to thin crescents and only slowly opened. Then tears began.

He wanted to repeat to her what Dostoevsky had told Smerdyakov about the condition under which anything was permissible but why waste that on her? So he asked. Suppose the Superintendent had found out about my staying here during the Philadelphia trip?

He knew. She sniffed and quit squirming.

He didn't believe her. She said it was so: Indeed he was in Philadelphia at the time with your grandmother. She said she thought he knew they were lovers: it was what they did every time (she spoke in gasps) every time that they sent him to visit with his teacher. And the rule she said in squeaks Is love. He became aware that he was working at her vigorously and that her middle was making a ruck sound: ruck ruck ruck. She was bent over his arm. He withdrew and she straightened a few degrees.

He wiped on a handkerchief and then stood and told her to stand and to follow him. He led her into the bedroom which till then he had never seen: it was a particularly feminine place done in soft blue and pink and otherwise white. Knickknacks were laced liberally about and the effect was collegiate. But the teddy bears and caps and toys were more childish than even a playful collegiate would allow: they were her trophies from her boys. He had not seen the room even when he stayed with her for that week during the war but instead she had fixed a place for him on the couch. Now he saw why.

Take off your clothes.

She looked stupidly up like a sheep and then fumblingly began to obey. He watched clinically as the garments came off and decided he had never seen anything as unerotic. She wanted to fold each piece and then put it away carefully but he denied her that and took her stuff from her and draped it on a puffy cerise wing-backed chair. She stopped when she got to the essentials and he stepped in back of her and undid her brassiere out of which fell two small footballs. There happened to be just such a miniature ball on a chest of drawers: made for the hand of a small boy. Whose was this?

She glanced but said she didn't know. She was looking away and covering herself with crossed arms. In the corner was a ball bat: did she recall the owner of that one? No. How about the airplane that someone skilled had put together? No. Did she put it together? No.

Again he went behind her and there he pulled down her last covering. She stood in it like a puddle. When he got around in front of her she made with her face averted rather an absurd parody of September Morn. Kitsch. If kitsch could be parodied: how could anyone parody a parody? While she stood so he went through the drawers and found at last what he sought: a collection of boys' garments. She couldn't identify them either. Nothing of his was there that he could remember so he asked what she had of his. She didn't know. He took her arm she had used the hand of to cover the small patch of moss and led her by it toward the bed and then twisted it to turn her onto it. Whose cap was it on the bed post he asked while loosening his buckle: it was a round one with a small bill of the sort popular before his time. He took it off the post and fitted it on himself like a yarmulke then pulled the covers from under her and got in beside and then on top of her and pulled up the quilt. She jerked her face sharply away from him and under the flaccid shielding arms laced over it he could still see the grimace. She was crying in wrenching and torn sobs but he was not deterred: Whose he asked Whose? Whose? Whose? Then he relaxed except for his supporting elbows and heard her say from a face like the mask of tragedy that it was her son's.

Then it was her turn to relax.

He hadn't known about a son. Yes she said she had had a son: he had died when he was ten. She thought everyone knew. No he said No one knew. He expressed regret and she accepted it. He asked the boy's birth date and she said nothing though her eyes were searching beneath her closed lids. I don't know she said I guess I've blocked it out. He said Sure and then excused himself and went to the bathroom. He was tired when he came back and said that with her kind permission he would stay until just before dawn. She nodded. He remembered and replaced the cap on the post and asked did she prefer to go to the couch as he had done before. She made no response and after a moment he noticed that she was asleep and breathing regularly. He found her electric alarm and set it.

He soon slept as well as she until a whine bothered him and he reached for the clock but with his arm bent upward and reaching realized it was bagpipes and that he was dancing. In swirling snow he was kilted and dancing and his grandmother in a long tartan was dancing a fling as was the Superintendent and yes his father and his Indian wife as well and even Mrs. Mowen. Everyone he had ever known was dancing to the skirling pipes and turning and turning like figures done by a Scottish Breughel but especially his grandmother: Dance she cried out of him Dance Buckley! Dance! Dance!

So dance he did until his arm completed a downward arc and shut up the alarm that was only then warming up to buzz. He sat up and remembered Mrs. Mowen beside him: she slept with arms crossed over her quilted breast. Waxen she was and with her mouth primly shut looked fixed for her coffin. The smell of deep sleep was upon her and therefore he supposed upon himself. He made his way to the bath for ablutions then dressed quietly without waking her and checked the refrigerator for juice. He liked orange juice to start his day but found none. There was a can of V8 in the cupboard and though it was warm and sticky he drank it and found what he thought to be bagels in the bread box. He'd never actually seen one before but took one along and pulled and chewed at it on his way out.

The paperweight he pocketed: that of course was the souvenir she had from him. Well he had it now. She was lying most certainly about the boy. It was unlikely she had even been married.

The air filled his lungs sharply and he enjoyed the mauve colors of a winter dawn. Pearl snow turned creamy then to a sort of orange bisque until the scene became one that might appear on the cover of a first class magazine except such journals seldom did middle-middle class subjects. People who read those magazines did not like to be dragged down by that sort of thing.

Then came the sun and he knew before he looked that he would see for that latitude something extraordinary and surely enough there were however momentarily two of them paralleled just above the horizon.

Hage, the Blue-Eyed Indian

Camel Dung said the Prophet said Jens Hage who added sagely Horseshit being unknown in those days. It was vintage Hage (rhymed with Soggy) and I thought of him for the first time in years as I stood quietly in front of a urinal in the remodeled bathroom of the fraternity house I had graduated from decades before. (The fraternity was my college and not Rabbit Warren U: at RWU I spent a few hours each day but I lived at the fraternity.) I looked quietly for the room where Lynn and I made out discreetly (there being no open visitation in those days) and found it was now a small dorm where four men slept while the curtains played before open windows in the cooling after-midnight air. These and others in residence likely were only a few of them under-graduate brothers to whom I would be a reliquary curiosity and even-tually an embarrassment: most of them probably were doing summer degrees. Teachers. No matter. I hadn't come to see them anyway.

Lynn who was long and lithe and possessed of what I called the most lovely hands this side of heaven had taken her hands thence two months past. Our children had long known of the event to come but couldn't attend the send-off. But they were okay and I was early retired. The undertaker had restored the breasts a surgical team had taken but no help was needed with her folded hands though they were slightly desiccated. They were laced with her confirmation beads. That's what I remember: hands. Hage's were short and quite pink like the rest of him. He was still about: I had seen him on TV.

The library downstairs was largely the same though I missed the old beer company print of the Custer Massacre. Lynn and I went there too when we could find nowhere else: neither of us was bothered by cavalrymen losing their hair. There still weren't many books but just some phonograph records dusty in a corner from long disuse and a couple of scrapbooks I didn't recall. No one would notice my light in that alcove so I sat and lit a cigar. By my senior year when I moved out of there and more or less in with Lynn it had seemed unspeakably banal—a portion of juvenilia to be left in the outgrown past except for parties which I still attended. Even so it was from the House that I considered that I had graduated. That was the same summer I put small strips of tape on each shoulder when we went to the beach so that when I tanned I would have bars there. I had the world by the tail: a degree a commission and Lynn tall and blonde. I picked through the records.

They were old not even remotely new. Old when I was enrolled there though I didn't recall them. Some were World War II things about Johnny Got a Zero and I Came Here to Speak for Joe and Coming in on a Wing and a Prayer. They were before me though I had heard them often enough as a kid but they were after and then before Hage who was there both before and after the War. And there was one called The Big Apple. In the scrapbooks were folk who looked about the same as my group or even those around when I came back for grad school but I didn't know any. Until in the corner of one glossy photo also labeled in careful script The Big Apple I saw Hage.

A very young Hage wearing saddle shoes and corduroys. It occurred to me that most of the young men and women in the book were dead or soon would be: Lynn was dead and we were nearly twenty years later than these. Surely many of them didn't clear World War II. Just the right age to be junior officers. Someone named Wallaby or called Wallaby who went down at Ploesti was someone Hage had liked and talked about a great deal. Maybe he was the guy doing The Big Apple with his girl. Hage's time was in what he called the CBI and in the Red Ball transportation unit which he said was except for him mainly black. He liked blacks though not as much as he liked Indians.

This was before Civil Rights and his taste was written off as an eccentricity of no note among all the other Hage eccentricities. When I first met Jens Hage I was a freshman and he was a fifth or sixth year senior and the last WW2 leaf left on the tree: I ran into him again in graduate school—I was in graduate school. He was still a senior or maybe back to being a junior—and then one more time that I will mention.

The first time was in the latrine at the fraternity house: I was shaving as I did once a week then when a blond crewcut came in and standing back toward me while facing the urinal on the opposite wall said Camel Dung etc. and then asked if he could borrow five dollars. It occurred to me by the time he was at the shaking and tucking stage that he was talking to me since no one else was in there except for someone in a stall whose shoes I did not recognize: then I saw that it was Campbell when his head appeared and looking quickly at the blond and then at me shook his head fiercely and mouthed an emphatic NO. Campbell was a senior who would shortly be off to Naval OCS which confused things: as a senior he had clout but as one would soon be leaving he left me as a pledge vulnerable to this man who apparently was an upperclassman and active.

If I had five dollars I'd sit up all night and watch it I said. It was a line my father had used often though generally in regard to larger sums.

The crewcut laughed at that and zipped and then extended his hand: Yentz Hage: I've been here longer than anyone else. Then he stood at the sink next to me and washed his hands. I told him that in Montana we washed our hands before rather than after since we didn't want to get our privates dirty.

An immediately interested pink face presented itself up to me—his head came about to my arm pit—with the round eyes of electric blue that only Scandinavians have. He wanted to know what part of it I was from and was disappointed to learn it was a Western part not near reservations. I mentioned the Blackheads and Flatfeet who weren't so far away and that perked him up though he didn't find it funny. Campbell flushed and came out of his stall then and went to the sink on the other side of me to wash: he and Hage said nothing to each other or anything at all except when Campbell was departing he turned and mouthed another No that Hage couldn't see.

Since I was a pledge coming in out of season (at mid-year after a false start at another school where the basketball coach didn't like me) I was an oddball and thus like the new boys who came into our grade and high school from time to time: temporarily oddballs themselves it meant the people most likely to seek their friendship were those who were permanently oddballs. Oddballs at either end of the spectrum: either too smart and thus square or else too dumb and thus square. Unless they were athletes and then of course dumb didn't count. Then as the new boys got to be known and sorted out they found themselves moving into this group or that invariably leaving behind the lost balls who had originally sniffed them out: probably the lost balls were used to it.

It was even so with Hage who sniffed me out. It was flattering for a while to kick around with someone north of thirty rather than south of twenty—someone who had been in the CBI theatre in the War and who had been in college for quite some time. His GI Bill was used up but he found it easy enough to exist as a lab assistant and by living in the Little Bohemia every residential college of any size always throws up especially if it has a graduate school. And from time to time he would come by his old fraternity to scrounge a meal or borrow five—never repaid—and now and then he would get lined up. But less and less as the variance in age grew and as his old vet buddies sobered up and one by one graduated and married and went to work. He had never married but had a girl friend even then. She was Jewish which he liked although he would have preferred that she be Indian. I never saw him with her though one night when he had invited me out for coffee (for which I paid) he pointed her out as half of a couple of girls who already had about them what I would later recognize as the patina of graduate school. At the time I noticed only the purple and green highlights playing off the oil of their hair.

Hage seemed unsure at first whether to go over and then he got up and went. The other girl made room and I slid in beside her but Ruth didn't shift: probably he'd borrowed five once or twice from her too. The other girl said of course I knew Ruth and she was Maggie McBride and I said then that now I knew Ruth and thanks. Ruth made a pleasant if vulpine acknowledgment and ignored Hage. As for Hage he said he liked Irish girls. Maggie said her family had been American since the potato famine and thus hardly still Irish and anyway she was half Jewish: she straightened as she spoke and I saw that she was something like five feet fourteen—the reason no doubt she'd moved over for me. She was slim and okay except for a wart about where Abraham Lincoln had one.

Hage stood there and told Ruth by way of farewell that he'd be leaving soon for the reservation: he was going up to attend some dances and he thought he might be staying for a while. Ruth gave every impression that she could bear the separation however lengthy. Hage tried to impress on her that it might be lengthy indeed. Ruth took both his hands in hers and looking up (but not much) said Umph. Hage flushed and moved for me to come away with him but it was not decisive enough that I had to go and when Maggie clamped my arm I stayed. I didn't see him for a while after that.

Why him want to be Indian asked Maggie who I learned was doing a degree in Jewish Studies and wanted to be a Jew. Him want to sleep in tepee Ruth answered. Him want to hump buffalo I said.

Hunt buffalo said Maggie Hunt. Ruth said Maggie didn't know Hage as well as we did. Then charitably she said that for some reason unfathomable to her he identified with Indians. Maggie wonder if he was an ANTH major. No he was in CHEM and wasn't good with people at all but typed them said Ruth e.g. Irish girls. Oh said Maggie. I began to wonder if I was there. After the waves of their chattering slid into a trough I spoke: He says he's like Moses and identifies with the oppressed. Ruth wanted explication. I had heard—in class of course— that Moses (Cf. Mose) was perhaps an Egyptian perhaps the illegitimate son of Pharaoh's daughter. Lots of people do that sort of transference I said. When I told Hage about it that's what he had told me: Lots of people. Of course he already knew Moses wasn't born Jewish. Ruth said Sure and advised me not to believe all my teachers: she said they were in the main old Hages.

I saw little of Ruth after that for awhile too except as I would run into her because of Maggie who had developed a keen interest in basketball and who came sometimes to freshman practice. I decided that if Ruth was as much of a girlfriend as Hage had or had ever had then maybe he ought to have considered becoming an Indian a long time before: what was more likely was that like odd balls everywhere he had never known any other response and thought it was what everybody got.

As for Mag's Jewish background I couldn't discern it (if indeed I had known what to look for) she even giving no credence to the theory (endorsed by Hage) that the Irish were one of the Lost Tribes. She planned to take her summer in Israel in part to learn the language and in part to identify herself more fully with a nation that she said was a force for good. She said it would mature me if I went too—maturing being something she felt I badly needed at the time—though I was inclined to gain it through the gradual accretion of years.

I could tell she was sometimes distressed by my underclassmen gaucheries and I tried not to repeat them. She meanwhile hung on since she felt she needed someone. (This was a long time ago remember.) So she put up with me. Once when the two of them were together I suggested she take Ruth to Israel instead. Mag was glad I had said it and Ruth was not glad: she was Not Religious and didn't go in for that excrement. She didn't know Shavout from circumcision and further- more did not give a damn. Unintentionally I had driven a wedge between them and found myself drifting down on the side of Ruth. So when Mag went off on her dig or whatever I came to see more of Ruth. And once again of Hage.

Hage had said he liked Ruth because her Jewishness looked a trifle Indian and he considered Joseph Smith likely correct on the Indians being one or more of the Lost Tribes. Apparently Hage thought Jews had a very bad sense of direction. Maggie countered that Smith had solved all the pressing theological problems and not a few scientific ones of the early nineteenth century as indeed anyone might then as

72

now by writing Science Fiction. But Maggie was long gone. Ruth and I were a sort of couple—I was her find she said—while Hage bore me no ill will especially when he found an Indian girl the very next week. Mona something. She as most people were also was taller than Hage and was much rounder. He liked her because she was Indian. Indeed nothing would do but that we all double-date.

The first thing noticeable when Mona and Ruth were seated side by side was that Ruth in no wise looked Indian: her face was lupine as I said but sweetly lupine. Sidelong glances I recall that she gave me showed forty or so teeth to a side—the better to eat you with she grinned—while Mona's face was simply lunesque. Seeing Mona Short Whale from the side was like trying to see the moon from the side which of course it hasn't got one of: perfectly round. Perfectly round though her face was it like the moon (a red moon said Ruth a hunter's moon: Umph!) also could be seen shadowed so that you saw only a slice of it. But then one had to guess at the features the way one guessed at them on the moon. Her skin was pocked and also lunesque in that regard.

Also Mona was dumb as owl turds, but she was Indian, so Hage liked her. I had thought at first when he introduced her that he had said she worked in an Alcoholics Rehabilitation Center but gradually it came to me that she lived there. They had let her out so she could see Rashomon which Ruth had also wanted me to see as part of my tutelage so there we were. Well I said in reference to Mona Big Moon's grumped comment that she would rather have gone to a musical Well it's not one you walk out of humming a tune. Ruth smiled one of her wolfish delights and stretched up to nuzzle my neck which was something I recalled that superior canines did to lesser ones just to let them know they could tear out a throat or two if they wanted. She said that wasn't the fault in it at all and nuzzled again.

In the bar we all ordered large beers with me put in the darkest corner since I hadn't any ID. I didn't get checked because the others were so obviously of age and also because the waitress was absorbed in the pairing of Hage and Two Dogs Humping. Ruth wanted me to understand that what was wrong with the film was not that it was Oriental but

73

that it wasn't Oriental enough. Hage said Orientals understood that we are one with Nature and that we forget it at our peril. Mona said nothing. Hage offered it that Indians were prime examples of this and didn't she agree? Mona was setting down her tankard which she had emptied in one draft and except for indicating her desire for another was impassive.

That much was ordered and Ruth smiled something about those who found the Cultures of Others to be Interesting so long as they didn't have to be part of them themselves: It's why History is so charming to read and so dreadful to live she told just for me: Pleasant from the outside if you don't have to suffer from actually being there. I had just declared a History major since I had to declare something. The difference between Jens and you she told me Is that your nostalgia can never be disabused.

Hage turned a little red though less than he would have liked: It's not nostalgia with me. If it were I would want the Old Norse gods who incidentally aren't so different from their Indian cousins only less sophisticated. But it makes no difference my not being Indian: the greatest leaders of suffering people aren't always biologically of them. Ataturk was an Albanian DeValera was American and half Spanish at that Churchill was half American Stalin wasn't Russian—then he paused to search a pocket with the uncounting hand for money for the beer. I gave it and Ruth glared at me and Hage extended his little finger and thus used up that hand: Napoleon wasn't French Hitler wasn't German—I'm not saying all these people were oppressed really but they were being held back in some way. Mona was the while drinking from the pitcher without offering anyone else any. With it nearly gone she paused and smiled at me. Thanks for the beer I guess. Hage continued: They were taking people back to the Old Gods. The Old Gods aren't dead you know they're not even Gone.

Ruth thought it funny he was so keen on certain old gods and on Indians going back to them: when whites went back to old gods we tended to call it Fascism. Mona finished the pitcher and belched softly but thoroughly. She seemed to be approaching a separate peace and I wondered how women seemed not to have to empty their bladders so often as men. The place was filling up and thickening with cigarette smoke which back then I liked secondhand: atmosphere.

Ruth and Hage went at it about Cultures and I flagged the waitress who nodded and eventually brought another pitcher which I paid for and was careful to share about before passing the last half to Mona. At the time I could not recognize Ruth's and Hage's as a familiar argument that familiar people established and then brought up from time to time when they wanted to fight though I later learned about it after I married Lynn. It was something that Marital and Philosophical arguments have in common: people pick their favorites in both categories—often making their reputations by doing so—and then when they want a fight (or reputation) they bring them up and when they or others are tired of it they by mutual consent let it die. No philosophical arguments are ever solved. Philosophical arguments like marital arguments are only brought up from time to time and then when the need that caused their re-issuance is satisfied they are let drop and set aside until the next time. Marital arguments are solved only by death never by divorce though in the case of either frequently are replayed once a survivor finds the proper replacement disputant to pair off with. Lynn did that with her second husband. Of such is love.

The evening at the bar ended when Mona finished the last pitcher and slumped into a corner on her side of the booth and began ever so perceptibly to slide under it: when Ruth yanked me out of the booth she shoved Hage back down on his side of it and against Mona Over-the-Hill who rose perpendicular for a moment like the Titanic before its final plunge and then like the ship quickly disappeared taking Hage down with her. His head reappeared only briefly after it sank below the table the first time: And Jesus wasn't Jewish!

Then a hand reaching up for salvation caught his collar and took him downward instead. Ruth cursed all the way back to her digs. I pretended to listen. An occasional assent was all she required and I wondered instead on the likes of her and of Hage and all such sorts. They were intellectuals who had got that way by reading other intellectuals: Ruth and Hage were only Followers but what if they got really good at it and started a Movement all their own? They would be like the writers I had been hearing too much about in Lit class who so much admired Hemingway that they wrote parodies of him. It ought to have embarrassed Hemingway but I don't think he ever spoke to it.

Even so with Great Intellectuals: Dostoevsky saw it and illustrated it with Ivan and Smerdyakov with Ivan's follower doing what his half-brother had only implied. A much better illustration than his Grand Inquisitor and Christ. Nietzsche (and maybe Darwin) maybe had Hitler as a Follower though others say Hitler wasn't smart enough to understand him (them) but of course that's the point.

And Christ (the non-Jew?) had the most Followers. Of all people didn't He realize what would happen? And if He didn't then didn't the Father know what was involved? Look at it: the first thing that came of the Incarnation was the Massacre of the Innocents. Jesus did say He came to bring a sword—but to kill babies? Lessers like Marx with their Lenins and Stalins and Maos don't bother so much. But Jesus should have known better. Or maybe He did and my questions were wrong. And Ruth went on giving answers.

It had rained while we were in the bar and the night was delicious: she lived just outside Bohemia and we went on wet sidewalks past picket fences patterned by a shawl of leaves cast by the streetlight over silver streetcar tracks glistening in the rain. The single leaves floated black hearts over her dress and she quit cursing long enough to work her key. Her landlady she whispered didn't allow visitors after ten so we would have to be quiet: also I would have to stay till the woman left the next morning around nine. Okay?

On that softest of nights? I would have been receptive to a moderately pleasant grizzly bear nervous though I was with Ruth's heavenly gates opening before me. Okay.

Inside there was a snoring lump in a large chair smelling of urine or else the chair was all right and the woman smelled so. Landlady. We crept along on floors so worn there was a runnel down the middle and then Ruth stepped on the tail of a cat. The cat screamed in a marked

Chicago patois and the landlady slept on. Still we were silent till we got to the back room which was Ruth's. Then she talked again. I hadn't realized in those days the tremendous value intellectuals put on words and how they needed to talk themselves into everything even love.

But she had to do it—to go over everything that she had been over with Hage only this time he was unmistakably named Glaucon and served only to set her up. I had already decided after a half term of Intro to Phil that Glaucon probably won every damn one of the arguments the first time around and that Plato had just written the debates so that Socrates won. The Prof said that might have been so but (1) probably Plato was trying to copy the leading literary genre of the day (drama) and thus made it a dialogue and (2) he said that the Unwritten Word is as Smoke and such was the value of written discourse: it simply didn't matter who won the unwritten debates. (I ask you to believe that I have been honest in what I have written here.)

The only thing that she gave Hage was that yes Jesus according to both the Jerusalem and Syrian Talmud she had heard (from Maggie) was not Jewish but rather the offspring of a Syro-Phoenician woman and a Roman. Named Panterra which was an insult since it meant All the Land—there was possibly a List of Suspects then and no more than. Then she smiled her wonderful teeth at me and began to nuzzle. It was my first but she knew the terrain and guided well and offered compliments while raving at herself for having forgotten the capabilities of seventeen-year-olds.

Then she forgot them again and then forgot me and I seldom saw Hage again even in what was left of Spring Term. Though there was one last meeting over coffee (I paid) when he told me that in Physics pattern is all: molecules and solar systems looked alike for that reason and were not necessarily interchangeable although he wasn't perfectly sure we weren't only a fart blown out the asshole of a giant yes it was possible. But only if the giant himself was a very small item on one of our puffs of flatus. I didn't follow that one and have wondered if I got it right.

Then I lost track of him as well as of Ruth and of course of Maggie though much later I ran into her not as a perennial graduate student but as an academic secretary who was the perennial dater of graduate students. Or so I heard she was. In my Junior year I met Lynn who was a Sophomore at the time. And so on. Hage I saw by chance on television when the American Indian Movement was momentarily featured and there he was in denim and badges and such. He mentioned the hundreds of broken treaties and was arguing their right to sign leases to allow strip mining on their reservation.

Maggie on last meeting had hyphenated her name to Malone-McBride by picking up her mother's maiden name. She looked oddly at me when I said Malone didn't sound Jewish and became hostile when I pointed out it was only her mother's father's name. She had barely recalled me and didn't remember Hage at all. Ruth she recalled but had her confused with someone else and perhaps was merging the personalities. And her wart had a whisker in it. So much for the past.

I closed the book of party photographs. It was a collection that had ended ten years before I had shown up on campus. I put it away except for the one with Hage in it which I stole. I tried sleep on the couch near where Lynn had first confessed her love for me but I found sleep impossible. Well before the time when one can know another I gave it up took my photo and went on my way.

Go, Purple

Harry put on his letter sweater when he went out to rake the leaves in part because leaf-raking and burning meant Fall and his letter had been in football and that was played in the Fall and he wore it partly because it was colored purple and gold and so were many of the leaves: it made him feel more united with things—both with Tradition and with Nature. Tradition was what held things together: football in the Fall and then baseball got you through the summer. Basketball he could take or leave alone. Church at Christmas and Easter were good: red and green for the former and yellow and lavender for the latter: if they came up with something in orange and black for Halloween he'd go then too. Tradition and Nature.

Unities were hard to come by these days so he always wore the sweater when he raked leaves. After forty years it was out at elbows and the bottom border was becoming raveled but he was happy as he put it on again. He pulled tight his tweed cap and stuffed and lit his pipe. In a sense he was burning leaves there too.

His house was something that could be called a bastard Queen Anne in brick with a little stucco and a sun porch to the side and a chimney in the middle. There were baked red tiles on the sun porch floor and he liked it very much but his wife put too many plants there especially in the winter. This also was the time of year the calico cat preferred to sun herself there instead of getting in by the fireplace where she of right belonged. For what did one search out a calico cat

79

anyway if not to put before the fireplace? A calico cat with a grandfather clock and a fireplace and you're set for the winter. And in the Fall you rake leaves.

That was one reason he had been keen on buying the house—the leaves (or rather the trees)—and the other reason had been the sun porch. His wife liked having a second floor sewing room. She knit as well as sewed and she had made a fine afghan of autumnal browns: it was on the large and comfortable living room couch even then waiting for him and he would be pleased to nap there when the raking was done: it was his own nest of leaves.

There was a bite in the air already but it took only a little raking before he was warm enough. As soon as possible (there were as yet few leaves) he made a fire and sat and looked at it and enjoyed the smokes that came from it and from his pipe. A haze began to form and drift down the curving two lane road that had been laid out in just post-revolutionary days and occasional cars slumbered down it. In another week the college football games would begin and he looked forward to it. He had married early and retired early but he had always saved and now the house was paid for and the cars and there was usually some left over at the end of the month. He raked up two more piles and burned them and then went in for his nap. After first taking off his shoes (but not the sweater) he pulled the afghan over him. Melchizedek who had been named before they knew her sex or that all calicos were female joined him there and cuddled between his legs. Marge he could hear humming away at her sewing machine upstairs when he first drifted off like smoke from a fading fire. He woke when he heard her doing things in the kitchen but decided to sleep some more and let himself sink back down out of his bones. It was dusk when he finally awoke.

He didn't need glasses but he had to focus a couple of times before he was sure of what he was seeing. When he made out what it was he nodded All Right to them and waved them on away from the window and toward the front porch. Seeing there were three of them he looked about to see what Marge had prepared: apparently nothing. He managed to locate an apple in the dining room table centerpiece then got a candy bar out of the cabinet and found a quarter in his pocket: he opened the door where they were waiting and gave them out in order to the corpse the skeleton the ghost. They hesitated about taking them but on seeing he had shut the door they took off. He yawned and picked up his shoes to carry upstairs and put in the closet in exchange for his slippers and went up to empty his bladder and refill his pipe just once before dinner. The evening paper had come and he got it when he came back down and went out to the sun porch to read it. Marge came drying her hands into the living room looking for him. She still had the basic shape she had when they married except that was about a half-inch layer more of it all around. That was satisfactory: she had gained it after menopause. Except for being skittery she had taken that well enough.

Well Harry who was it? She kept wiping her hands though they should have been dry enough by then.

Kids trick-or-treating. He finished skimming the first page and went directly to the comics.

Well they're a little early aren't they?

He guessed so. Had she bought anything for them to give? For use when more of them came as surely they would? She didn't answer him at all but only stared at him a while and then went back to prepare dinner. He called after her to make some cookies and she said she would. Good: cookies would do them nicely. He finished the funnies and turned to sports. He saved editorials till last except for local news and obits. Maddeningly he found a two-column piece on leaf burning and complaints about such as a hazard to health. The City Council had taken it up at the suggestion of as Mrs. Someone he didn't know but felt he ought to. Marge knew her too but couldn't recall who she was: it would come to her. For the time being the motion to ban had been tabled. Damn do-gooders.

Half way through dinner they were there again. But it was not another bunch it was the same three. He gave them three bananas from the centerpiece and also a scowl once he learned it was not another set. Marge said that next time she would get it if there was a next time. He didn't think they would brazen it but hadn't she better start the cookies since other surely would? She put down her fork and looked at him curiously till he asked what was up.

Harry: Halloween isn't for a month not for more than a month.

Then he put down his fork and stared at her. He picked it up again: Just kids Marge trying it out. You know.

They both began to eat again though slowly. The doorbell rang. He avoided looking up till it rang again and he reminded her that she had said she would take it the next time. But she didn't budge just kept on eating slowly moving the food up to her mouth chewing deliberately. The bell rang one more time then quit. They had coffee and she made cookies. There was nothing on TV that they wanted but they watched anyway after first pulling down the shades and locking all doors as was usual.

The next morning Harry was unable to sleep and got up and cooked breakfast and asked whether she intended to go to Church. Maybe: she didn't know. He said he would if she would.

Why? It's three more months until Christmas.

Don't get smart Marge you're not exactly a pillar yourself.

She said she went very often indeed. Actually it was one Sunday in four or five. But they both went that Sunday and she fretted throughout. She was nervous at having him along. He sat and tried to make sense of it but was unable to follow even with the help of the program: they'd changed the book and he resolved he'd not come again but was glad afterwards he had gone. Except for all the people he vaguely knew who make half-jokes about his presence. And the minister had changed: this one was a young snuffy with curly blond hair and an intense look about him. He'd spoken about Death and Hope but it was boring and Harry tuned out. Snuffy was built like a football player though. It was his wife who had asked for the leaf-burning ban.

The week passed slowly. The thing to look forward to was the beginning of the season on Saturday: indeed it was a game between the Purples and some Eastern team but was scheduled for delayed viewing. That irritated him: why couldn't the Purples' game be live and the other game be delayed? Because of who had bought the advertising rights he learned but still he festered.

As it happened the Purples' game was live on radio but he refused to listen. Marge in trying to be helpful started to tell him the halftime score and he snapped at her. After that she went back to the kitchen and clattered about and then went up and ran her sewing machine. He was tempted to turn on the radio and find out how they were doing in their opener against the East Coast and to help resist it he put on his letter sweater and got out the bike to pedal the five or so blocks to the local grocery for his snacks for the game. At the epicure counter he got some really good Muenster cheese some salami and gourmet crackers. The beer he had at home so he paid and left but caught a ravel from the right elbow on the door latch. He would have to be careful. By the time he got home and got his plate fixed it was time.

It seemed the real thing but wasn't: it was close and well played and the crowds shouted and were now delighted now furious but Harry kept recalling that it was all over. He didn't know the outcome but everything that would happen had happened: each sprain each paper cup thrown down and crushed in grandstand fury even each blade of grass that bent. All of these as well as the red dogs the fumbles the passes and sneaks these also were known. At the half the Purples held a tenuous three point lead after a brilliant series of plays and a last minute field goal. But he was depressed. When the half time marching out began and the bands started making cartwheels and designs that had been worked out by some by-taxes-paid idiot weeks before and which they'd been practicing nearly as long—when this happened he was depressed. Then there was a Queen of some sort wheeled out in a Cadillac and her escort who was a reedy callow youth dressed in a white dinner jacket helped her ascend the lathing and crepe paper throne. A microphone whined and she told them all that this was the happiest day of her life. Marge came in to see that: she had been Queen when he had been Captain and she began to munch the crackers and cheese. While she watched the crowning and giving-of-roses she carefully peeled off a layer of salami that needed no peeling. He hated that but he recalled the Spring night after he'd first got his sweater.

He asked her if remembered that night and the '33 Ford with the rumble seat. His smile made her think he might have something on his mind and she got up to go: she said if he took off the sweater she would put some elbow patches on it some leather ones she'd bought. He pretended to do so and then took her hand and she said No but he had her and amidst protests she backed to the couch. She said she wanted to go to the bathroom first but he wouldn't take a chance on her not returning and she said Oh all right. All he did was take off just enough and she did the same. That was the way it had happened that letter sweater night forty years earlier except then it was only a rumble seat and not an ample couch with an afghan. It was the old warmth though and he was pleased as always to put on her warm little mitten which still was only a generous quarter-size too large.

When play resumed he found that he really didn't give a damn who won: it was planned anyway. He reached down to turn it off and bending down to do so began to wonder if that action of turning off the TV had also been pre-recorded. He straightened up sharply and got back to his chair in time to see the quarterback shake off a tackler and get away his pass even as he had shaken off fate. But of course he hadn't—not any more than had the quarterback: it was pre-recorded that the football player would get away and it was pre-recorded that he would decide not to turn off the switch. The pass was intercepted.

So that was it. He sat back and let his head sink and put his feet up on the hassock and watched the way Napoleon was said to have done at Waterloo after his heavy cavalry bogged down. Marge went through the room on her way to the sun porch and doing a double-take asked if the Purples were losing. He didn't answer although it happened that they were winning. She went on out and resolved not to let that happen again in the early evening especially not at halftime break. He was getting too old and needed his sleep afterwards.

The cat came in and curious as usual looked up at him. No he said It happens that they're winning.

The cat shrugged and went on out to the sun porch with her mistress. He decided he would write the Stadium and cancel his usual

Thanksgiving Day tickets. While he was yet brooding thus in came Marge and unbuttoned his sweater and pulled it off first one arm and then the other and then yanked it from behind his back. She said something about elbow patches and by the end of the telecast she had it back with the border neatly repaired and the crisp new and unbendable elbow patches in place. He put it on and went out to rake leaves in the dark. The Purples had won but he might have known that easily enough simply by turning on the radio three hours earlier.

That night to Marge's surprise he found himself again interested and told her so. She was so unprepared for the approach that she allowed it even without thinking of anything to barter for in return. And thus it was for every night for a week and often during the days as well at unpredictable times so that she began to spend as much time out as possible and went to the grocery every day at least once and sometimes more. The pranksters had rung twice but they didn't answer the door.

Then when she got home one fine day when everything seemed to be orange and blue she saw a strange woman leaving the doorstep. Oh: it was the minister's wife. Who brightened when she saw Marge. Hello! she yelled as if just in from two years in Tehran: Your husband's not home I guess. Lucky to have caught you! She brushed away a forward-falling lock that poured back like chocolate. She had the teeniest of crow's feet just beginning to track around almond eyes: a candy bar going stale? In a tan college girl duffle coat over brown crew neck sweater.

Oh Harry's probably there Marge said If he isn't out back raking leaves. He just doesn't like to open the door sometimes.

Candy's mouth closed into a receding smile. She understood. Then she touched her lapel where there was a large black button with AD on it in orange: Well Marge I guess you wonder why I'm here.

So come in! Come in Candy! Marge started to move toward the door.

Oh no no no: I just wanted to collect for the cause she said and added softly that her name was Holly.

Oh yes Holly: she fetched out a five. Then she asked could she send a cheque instead—for Income Tax purposes That was how she kept the receipts. Always glad to give to the Church she said: Anno Domini?

Oh no no—nothing like that. Her eyes made tracks appear again: Cover Girl make up. She said no it was Abolish Death: We've decided to go for the top—beyond Cancer Heart Disease Senile Decay—everything. Her face now was hard.

Oh all right. I'll mail it to the Church. Or bring it with me. Just make it out to Anno-Abolish Death? Okay? She began to hurry in: Candy wanted to tell her all about it and she did not want to hear. Candy smiled and left. Not Candy she told herself: Holly.

Harry and Marge stayed on the sun porch the rest of the day with the door locked and the shades drawn. This time when he assaulted her she showed no reluctance at all and began desperately to urge him on. When it was over he noticed a weird tingling in his genitals which tingling he allowed to continue until he realized it was the cat sniffing at his scrotum. He disengaged immediately and Marge rearranged herself and fished a magazine out of the rack and began reading and he filled his pipe. The cat gathered herself back together after being so suddenly forced from the couch and then concerned herself with the cleansing of her whiskers and muzzle. Her muzzle was beginning to show almost all white. And how old was their cat? They got her when Marge began menopause and their decision not to have kids became moot. So they got Melchizedek as a sort of compromise. Now the cat was becoming less spry. Marge was still spry and her hair was not graying. His own dome was nearly bare.

Was there anything special he wanted for dinner that night? Steak tartare he said: raw beef steak ground and a thick slice of raw onion with a raw egg plus the usual spices. Plus coffee. Strong black coffee.

The refrigerator held everything he asked for. I'm going to the grocery Marge said: Why don't you go out and rake leaves? You haven't raked them in quite a while and they're all over the place even in the neighbors' yards.

He reached under her skirt and she slapped at his hand and left: he was becoming impossible.

As she pulled out of the drive way she saw him emerge with rake in hand and cap on head with pipe in mouth and his purple and gold sweater buttoned up his front. It was the best of all possible Fall days and she felt very proper in her town-and-country attire: pebble grained shoes and a plaid skirt such as you saw advertised in *Cosmopolitan* and her home-knit oatmeal colored cardigan she was glad she hadn't given to the church bazaar the last Spring. That was her committee—the Bazaar—and she got involved in it every April or May.

Parking was easy in the big asphalted grocery lot and since there was nothing in it for anyone to take she left the station wagon unlocked. Perhaps when the opportunity presented itself they would get an Airedale pup to replace their own dear Astra who had been dead for how long? A decade. No it was a decade and a half. And at that it was Astra II.

The Supermarket was decorated occasionally with orange and black Halloween things and there were a few corn stalks stuck at the ends of aisles and a heap of pumpkins was at the far checkout counter. She made a note to buy a pumpkin. Then she began to look about at the gourmet stand: it was the first thing you had to go by just as the candy bars were next to the cashiers. She bought some snails. Harry had got the trays for them years ago and the holders so all she needed was the can itself. And some garlic. They were disgusting things except when properly cooked. A child had she conceived one would have fixed itself to her that way and there would have curled up and grown. She noticed a trickle from her last set-to but it was slight. Oh Harry.

After a few minutes she left the gourmet counter and the condiment rack and went on to cereals and then to meats. She had put into her cart only the snails and the garlic but she had been worrying each item seriously before putting it back and she shuddered: grocery shopping was simply not that important. Then she rounded a corner and saw two women talking about a cake mix with the one assuring the other that the end result was moist and tasty and the icing was like velvet. So people really did talk that way. And what difference did a cake mix make? She passed by the coffee and snorted at the brand that was guaranteed to insure rape by one's husband. There were soaps that were supposed to elicit the same sort of male response. The toilet tissues spoke of tender love between oneself and one's fanny: voiding was chic. The meats had all been virile and lusty. The fresh salad vegetables were organized into healthy groupings of yellows greens orange green again then pink green again another orange and she began to feel vertigo. She held the cart tightly with her eyes closed until the floor got steady again.

The whole mess was insane with products that promised Love and Health and Excitement and above all Meaning—if only she would buy them. But there was no meaning: not in oranges nor in steaks nor in cake mixes no not even in toilet paper and vaginal deodorant. They were lying to her all of them. Above her head was stapled a poster of a deliriously happy family with all of them smiling like idiots: even the cat and dog were smiling. That one owed it all to a prune juice and persimmon mixture. The same poster must have been distributed to thousands of stores across the country and it had been designed by people who knew what they were doing.

And who believed it? No one—but a lot pretended. Liars she said and walked out. She left her cart standing there with its garlic and snails. She drove home jerkily and had to stop twice from dizziness and once she felt that she had to vomit but didn't. It didn't mean anything none of it did.

She said nothing of her malaise when she got home except to mention that she was going upstairs to rest a bit. Harry was waiting for a kickoff. She remembered that was the chief interest of people in Socialist countries too and in all the in-betweens: a different kind of football but football. For this Christ was incarnate? Probably He liked football too. From the top of the stairs she asked Harry's opinion.

What? Then he returned to the game where they had formed up and the quarterback bent over to sniff the center's rump. She gave up and turned to her room when the door bell rang. She waited for Harry to rise to answer it but he did not do so and she called down to him and he called back that she could get it if she wanted. She returned and took his hand and together they went to meet the pranksters. It turned out not to be them at all but only a salesman with his back to them. Before the pranksters had started coming either one of them would have tried to shut the door with a silent shake of the head but now they were pleased to admit someone. Then they saw it was a cleric.

It was their minister as it turned out. He'd been there only eight months and she hardly knew him but Harry did. He even had some questions.

But was he interrupting No said Harry Only the football game.

Oh that was good go right ahead: The uh family that cheers together uh adheres together. They all laughed at that and then stood there as if each had grown two extra arms. Then they went to the sun porch and Marge left to brew some tea. The minister sat on the cat but without serious injury to either. He was not long out of seminary and from a well-known one at that but he had since discovered no one in the parish knew of it or cared. His had been a moderately late vocation. Seeing a baseball on a stand curved like those made to receive a crystal ball he asked after it. He said he had played the game not too long ago.

Harry said it was a ball hit foul off a Christy Mathewson pitch in 1906 and the man seated next to his dad had caught it. He took it down and smiled as he rolled it around in his hands a few times while the minister looked appreciative. Then Harry handed it over: Here Mr. Campbell take it take it: it's yours.

The ball was like any other except maybe a shade lighter. Then when an attempt was made to hand it back Campbell was told no that it was his. Marge was back and seated and looked incredulously at Harry but he was adamant. But why didn't he want it anymore?

I just don't.

Then he glanced at Marge and back at the minister: You know what that means to me?

The cleric looked about to speak but was cut off: Nothing—nothing at all: ab-so-lutely nothing.

The old salt has lost its savor eh? He jostled Harry on the knee. That reminded Harry of the fellow Campbell had replaced: he had built up the parish with Scouts and ball teams and Bake Sales and Auxiliaries with suppers and bowling leagues and most who attended were pleased. Harry detested the man.

You feel that way too do you? The minister smiled a conspiratorial grin. Then he nodded and told them both that games were what we made up to control chaos. Time-binding. With rules: because maybe there aren't any rules still less an Umpire. But games give us something to do between Now and Then.

Then? Asked Marge.

Oh you know: when it's time to put on the wet bathing suit. Until then we have games. Of all sorts.

The minister clapped his knees and stood up and they rose at once to see him off. He hoped to see them in church that Sunday and both agreed they would be there. He got good eye contact and shook the hand of each and left. They promised again they would be there.

When he left they went back to the football game. Even the cat did. Harry brought snacks the crumbs of which he got on his sweater and both cheered from time to time. At one point Harry said He likes Notre Dame.

Marge wondered about the non sequitur then got it and laughed. But not BC?

Harry laughed and said Nope.

They went back to the game which the Purples won. Marge then went back to her knitting and Harry decided against raking and in favor of going to the secretary and writing cheques for all of the end-of-the-month bills which he stuffed into stamped envelopes and put in the mail slot for picking up at the next delivery. That wouldn't be until Monday.

It was getting cold indeed and a few flakes were coming down. Then they remembered it was Halloween: A bad night for the kids he said. Marge said she'd get some cookies ready and they went into the kitchen. They were just beginning to think about their own dinner when the bell rang. Harry slapped his hands flat on the table and said he would go: Head of the family you know.

She said she knew. Harry turned and asked But what if? She said in that case he was to invite them all in. She heard him go to the door but there was no sound for a moment or two and then she heard him suddenly jovial: Come in come in—right this way. We're been expecting you!

He was laughing and returning to her while behind him came dragging noises and she waited to see what it would be and what it would mean.

Don't Lose This, It's My Only Copy

I get migraines and to relieve them have a prescription that has for its major ingredient a vasoconstrictor called ergot: it's derived from a mold that grows on wheat in damp weather and some authorities believe that because 1690/91 was a wet one in Massachusetts it caused the hallucinations that led to the Salem Witch Trials the year following. That is if you have expanded veins (especially in your brain) then ergot is for you but it your veins are normal and you constrict them with ergot then you may see some strange things indeed. That may have been my condition a few days ago when I was poking through the ashes of our fireplace looking hopefully for a scrap or two of the best poem (in its only copy) I have ever written.

My wife had burned it the previous night she said because she thought it was only scrap paper and besides I should put up my stuff: I woke with what seemed a migraine (though they're not always there when they seem to be) and I took my ergot. I was short of the nausea stage but beyond that where it's difficult to focus or to stand to look at that on which you're trying to focus. One wing of the fireplace screen was closed and reflecting my sick face as I poked uselessly in the ashes through the open wing side. The face watched me and made as it says in the Psalms mouths at me: mocking talking jeering. I watched myself out of the corner of one eye and gradually registered the information that the reflection was full-faced while what I was presenting to the glass wing was nearly full profile. This is the sort of thing that is difficult to assimilate when one has a migraine.

I faced the visage but with my eyes closed. Summoning what was left of my rationality I opened and saw the face was pleased. Don't look it seemed to say: Don't look. Just mouthing words.

Don't look?

He shook his head in agreement and the act shook me: how can one shake Yes in agreement? It's like nodding No. Yet he did it. And was even then smiling. You have contributed to our archives he said And I thank you.

I was on hands and knees now and facing him. I had dropped the poker and suppose I looked like a dog. Archives?

Yes he said: This is how we get them—destroyed only (or last remaining) copies of manuscripts. Whether published or no: we get them when they are lost to you.

We I was aware of the pedantic ticking of the Edwardian clock on the mantel over my head: people with migraines notice (and hate) that sort of thing.

These are a sort of Spiritual Archives he said: We have the third part of Luke-Acts for example and also the third section of the Iliad-Odyssey and of course quite a bit of Sophocles. More in fact of Sophocles than you have. And an excellent book on the French Revolution by Carlyle.

I didn't know there was a third part of the Iliad-Odyssey (I did know about the lost portion of non-Scripture—lost before it could even be included): I've heard of Kazantzakis's addition to Homer I said But I didn't know there was a real one. By Homer I mean. I knew about JS Mill's maid.

The face closed its eyes in the smug manner of one learned in arcane matters when talking to the uninitiate: Oh yes it said. And we have a lot of Aeschylus too.

Then you have the complete set.

The eyes opened widely: No. The face saddened: We have only what is lost to you (much of it quite worthless—first novels and so on) so we have very few complete sets—although the destruction of the library at Alexandria yielded us great riches. Your poem will be a

94

worthwhile addition to a volume the Press is getting out soon. It's a collection of stuff from Younger Writers: You are under forty aren't you? I said I was and offered to burn some more—anything to get published. No he said they didn't print everything for circulation though of course they would be glad to look at it. However I had to understand that nothing could be returned and as of course I couldn't keep a copy—Heads you win, tails I lose. That sort of thing.

The face shrugged. (How can a face shrug? Get a migraine and find out.) Oh he said We do now and then lose things ourselves: some author whose work in question we are in possession of goes to a shrink (let us say) and through hypnosis they manage to recreate it—then it disappears from our files. Just as if we never had it. But we have Smith's first version of the Book of Mormon and Hemingway's ms that his wife lost in a railway station. Both of them are interesting.

But you have lost new stuff? Lots of it?

No not much: usually only when like your poem it gets burned. You see we have to wait until the ms decays. Decays beyond retrieval: dead. As with people. Of course we lose very few people.

Enoch and Elijah.

We never had them the face said. Not Mary either. About Jesus don't ask.

I got the feeling that the face was Jewish: a scholar. Lazarus I said Is the one I had in mind really. The face shrugged again. It is not a good experience to see a face shrug.

Listen he said I see that you are a Christian (from your poem I wouldn't know it) so I'll put it so you can comprehend it: it's like Purgatory where once you're there you've lost your Free Will. Stuff (like prayers from other people) can still come over from the Other Side but what you did there and what got printed there you leave behind. Also you don't get to write anything new: that's why we're so glad to get fresh items like this one of yours. We'll probably put it in an anthology or at the least it'll find a place in one of the quarterlies: each Circle has one. I asked what a Circle was. Circle he said. You know: like in Dante—a Circle of like-minded people. Naturally they publish for each other.

95

Then my parody of Lord Randall will almost certainly see print?

Pardon: Lord who?

Randall: it's a famous ballad. I detest ballads. The one you have is a parody of one called Lord Randall. Damnably he shrugged again: Don't know it.

"Randall Lord ate lunch at The Broth and Eels where this really neat girl worked the counter." That's how it starts I said. I remember that much. The face was in pain and mouthing stop but I went on. And the last stanza was something like His mother made his bed narrow and straight said "Heartburn," gave him Tums and Alka-Seltzer. When Barb phoned to break their regular date, Randy cursed, said "I hope that hell melts her."

It's no good now the face said It's only a fragment: with Sappho we can make do but believe me this one isn't worth it. You've just cut yourself out of a publication. And also something of your own composition to read when the time comes.

No matter I said: It'll all go to dust someday no matter what.

That's someday the face said Someday: between now and then what do you have?

Something to do to pass away the time between Today and Someday. Anyway as it is written in Ecclesiastes Of the making of great books there is no end And much reading is a weariness of the flesh.

Never heard of it.

Yeah Then how did you know of Dante?

We got the first draft: let me tell you he was glad of it when it came his time to cross over. Luke-Acts and Iliad-Odyssey I never read but I heard of them. Not Ecclesiwhosis though we have some Gnostic Gospels. For what they're worth. Which isn't much.

You're a scholar I said And like your words dead but I'm a writer and work for the living: especially do I work for those who will live in time to come. I write to make things real.

He shrugged again and would have waved a hand in dismissal at me had he had a hand to do so. I think maybe he waved an ear or partially did so. I don't care I said What they do in Hell.

Hell Schmell: this is Purgatory we're talking about.

So they read in Hell? What?

In Hell they do what they want to do. It's another story. I'm sorry: goodbye.

And he left and my migraine left and I recalled and finished the poem.

At the time—for a very short time—it seemed the best thing I had ever written or was ever likely to write. But that notion lasted a very little while and I was soon again discontent until I thought of something else to write about and make real.

The Grief of Terry Magoo

Terry Magoo had no gift for the Absurd so when the silicone job somehow went bad and there had to be a double mastectomy naturally he felt he was through as a topless go-go dancer. It was then that Juno had taken action: by God she would go on stage. She told Terry this when she brought up his breakfast tray of burned toast rubber egg and split level tomato juice. He picked at the food and tried not to look down as she talked to him. The bandages were finally off but he kept covered and did not want anyone (himself included) to see.

She could do it she said: she had taken ballet when she was five and kept it up till she was nine. He doubted the likelihood of success since she was 6' 3" and weighed 200: she was only abasing herself on his behalf.

You are doing it now she said straightening And so can I.

It was true and he knew it. Indeed he had shared a billing with several broad-shouldered hairy-chested fellows at the Club where he and Juno had met the year previous. No one had expected them to take up together still less stay together but they had. She straightened further and smiled down on him and he reflected anew how aptly she was named. All right he said I'll let you do it. But on one condition: I'll be your manager as well as your teacher. She smiled her acceptance and sat down at the foot of the bed thereby see-sawing him and his back pillow perceptibly higher against the head board. We can begin after breakfast. He stirred the juice absently with the stem of the fork until it began to homogenize and munched the char getting crumbs all over his pajama top. He came to a decision and clearing back his soft blond hair with one hand gestured a black wedge of toast at her with the other. Belly dancing he said decisively: That's the coming thing and you'll be a smash! As he spoke a fissure in the toast widened into a crevice and then a break occurred and a dark triangle landed in his lap. You'll have to shave of course.

She opened her shirt and checked herself out: quite a few. Okay she said. He sighed.

By phone he managed the booking and that gave them two weeks. Shortly after Christmas. Making her costume wasn't especially difficult since he had sewn clothes for her before. He'd never done her garments with such a feminine cast to them but it still was not much of a problem. Gauze pantaloons he ran from her bikini briefs down to her ankles where he gathered them into a two inch wide band that he covered with bangles. Rings that fit his fingers he put on her toes and from antique shops that had old coin collections he got enough tinkles to hang appropriately from her halter. Did the rest up in sequins and she was ready. Not the most graceful he'd ever seen but she tried hard and three days before she was to go on she could manage the stomach movements and shoulder shakes.

He was counting on her being somewhat different carrying her through. Like dancing bears at the circus: no one thought of bears as lyric creatures but that was what made attractive seeing them bounce about in tutus. The fact that they could be taught to do it at all. He heard a faucet run and despaired again: if only she wouldn't pee in the sink. All right he called to her Come on in and let's see the gyrations one more time. She trooped in wearing fatigues and a sweat shirt and performed at least as well as Bronco Nagurski could have.

But it wasn't enough. She had to go on three times. Once as a go-go dancer. That was okay: she knew the basic prances and jerks and she would get by all right. For boots to complete that outfit he had to go to her old Marine Corps boots but they would do all right if spit-shined. The problem was what to do for a third act. She would be on early and then again in an hour and a half and then hers would be the finale. If they made it—Las Vegas was next. He wanted Vegas so bad he could taste it. Never could have done it himself but Juno might. With his help.

He tightened his Chinese yellow robe around him and toyed with the grapefruit. He felt well enough to do the cooking again and he had an omelet coming up. Do your exercises he said and went downstairs to set the table. The plates rattled on the table as she flung her arms up and back then forward and down while her body listed from her hips with her legs scratching alternately like a chicken's after feed or a bull getting set to charge. Properly costumed the exercises would pass for go-go dancing. As soon as all was set he called up to her and the dishes settled into a slow rotation then suddenly plattered to a stop.

All right he shouted Come on down and eat and then we'll start work on your finale. She collapsed in the chair opposite and lurched suddenly over her plate. He calmed his glass of milk and passed her the ketchup she would want on her omelet. He might as well cook hamburger at every meal. She slopped it on and began to feed. If we make it big here he said I think we can get in at a place I know in San Francisco. From there it's straight to Las Vegas. Maybe a centerfold. He could hear her slow down her eating and he avoided looking up. Oh maybe not in Playboy he said but perhaps something like Esquire. You know.

Silence scraped across her plate. He continued to look at his. Although he said I don't know if San Francisco is such a good idea after all: Edgar Cayce you know says it's going to be destroyed soon along with New York City and Los Angeles. Really Chicago is about the only place of any size and importance that's safe to live in. Which I find a depressing thought.

No centerfolds.

Maybe for Cosmopolitan.

She chewed some more. Maybe she said. Just maybe. And I'll decide when and whether.

Of course he said Of course. Now you relax for a bit while I clear the dishes and watch Love of Life and after your lunch has settled and all we'll begin with your new dance sequence. I call it Venus de Milo. She grunted and went out to the back porch for a smoke.

Van's in trouble he said when she came back inside half an hour later. Juno had lived for a time with a girl named Jan and he knew it.

What about her?

Well her husband Bruce has this difficulty at City Hall and Van knows how to handle it but if she does it'll show she knows more than Bruce thinks she ought to and she doesn't know how to handle that. He chewed thoughtfully on an upside down thumbnail.

She sat down. Godam. So Jan had married. Of course here she was with Terry. But how did Terry know all this? How come you know so much about Jan's private life?

How come? It's on five times a week: you know I watch it faithfully.

She looked at him blankly and then realized. Oh: that Jan.

Van he said Not Jan. Let's start the routine. She said okay.

What we'll do he said Is drape you in a sheet and you'll sort of move gracefully around the stage and stop now and then in a classic pose. I'll fix you up to look like Venus de Milo. Only with a couple of things added.

Arms She pulled out a cigar sniffed it then replaced it. No he said No arms: what I'll do is put you under black light and then we'll put a sort of oh uh gloves on your arms maybe three-quarters of the way up and they'll disappear as it were (because of the black light) so you'll look very much like her indeed. She accepted this and he breathed easier. What he had to do after he found that no one made black three-quarter length gloves in her size was buy leotards and cut the legs off at the crotch: these would make one glove each for her. He was not in a hurry for that moment to come up either although it was entirely possible that she would accept that as easily as she had the rest of it. You just couldn't tell.

She undressed to her boxer shorts and he pinned the sheet about her standing on a stool to do the shoulders easily. Did she really look like Venus de Milo? Yes he lied. Actually she was a Michelangelo woman: a figure with a man's shoulders and thighs but with two hard tough protuberances of breasts stuck on. Then without telling her what they were he pushed her arms into the leotard legs. They fit well enough but of course the hands hung down like Idaho potatoes in the feet. Now he said Now you look like Venus de Milo. She smiled. He was pleased but was reminded of how Dr. Frankenstein must have felt when his creation suddenly took a shine to him. He opened the draperies and let the pearl and lavender glow of the winter day shine in.

Then he sat down and began to direct her. Now and then he said No no no no no and got up to make corrections and to show her how to shift about more gently. She was coming along nicely after a couple of hours when he saw something that made him wince: her sheet had sagged a bit and exposed a portion of her right buttock. On it was engraved some sort of device. What he gasped is that? She looked and saw nothing but the US Marine Corps insignia that had been a part of her for twenty-two years. He knew where she got her monthly pension cheque didn't he? Well yes of course but he didn't know the Marines did that to you. They didn't she said: I had it done in a tattoo parlor in Richmond. I was maybe eighteen. He collapsed deeply into his chair.

Then he sat upright. Of course: he would make capital of the tattoo and paint other things on her pseudo-graffiti so that she looked like a statue left out too long among the vulgar. She accepted that too: nervousness over the upcoming debut made trivial by comparison such minor improvisations as Terry was suggesting. She even accepted with no complaint his idea that since her navel was distended by the glass ruby they'd put in it for the belly dancing sequence—well since it was distended anyway probably she wouldn't mind having his gold pocket watch stuck in it for the de Milo turn. It was an heirloom from his father who had it from his father before him and so on for three or four generations. She would look like one of those Venus de Milo clocks see with this watch there in her middle. He toyed with the idea of a lampshade on her head but discarded it as going too far. And he said casually Of course you'll have to shave.

I did that she said and pointed between her un-swayable hemispheres.

Not there he said turning away and pointing: There. His back was to her and he was careful to keep it that way as he examined a book for the shelves. It was Cole. If she were to ask why he was studying it he would have no answer ready and impatiently he put it back as if that book was not the one wanted at all not at all. He sighed with hands on hips.

At length she spoke: I'm damned if I will.

Don't sweat it Juno. Everybody does it. They have to. It's part of the game.

It's not going to show anyway.

I know. Just do it. He heard no response except that presently she strode from the room in precise 36" military regulation steps as well as Harry S. Truman ever did. She said no more about it. And he dared neither to ask nor to look. But she practiced. And as the hour drew nigh she was increasingly ready. It wasn't her natural role: that much was obvious but it was also her charm. Then in the first week in January they made their way through the grey snow to the Coxcomb: half a block off what had been the busiest street in the city back after the war and before the suburban shopping centers began drawing off customers into branch stores. Now the branches were the main stores and those few quality places left down town were the branches. How he had loved those stores back then: especially at Christmases past when the best store had a series of displays in their series of windows and there were always moving parts. And inside! Glittering things in gold and silver and candy canes and wonderful smells from the perfume and cosmetics counters and the new and then (at certain pre-announced hours on certain days of the week) there would be choirs from the two or three good private schools for girls. Now there were no more choirs. Indeed there were few such schools: only one left and it let boys in. Thus were his thoughts as they picked their way down the well-lighted empty street. The Coxcomb could not have been there in olden days. Hotels had bands then and ballrooms. Now there were no hotels. Looking at the street he couldn't decide whether de Chirico or Hopper had painted it.

A walk-in restaurant was doing some business and they went in for coffee and to settle down. It too was a branch of a string of restaurants and drive-ins. She left on her duffle coat but when she set down the package with her costumes and stuff in them she offered to help him off with his camel's hair. He ran his hands through his hair both at once and sat down. She said she liked his suit. He smiled an Oh this old thing at her and picked up and then quickly put down his menu. He had on an apple green double-breasted with wide lapels over a mustard colored waistcoat and looked like an adolescent dressed for Cotillion: you could see the clothes weren't usual to him. Just coffee she said to the waitress. They were both nervous and neither wanted to confront the other with it so they stared into their cups.

They got to the Coxcomb early and went back to the dressing rooms. She had been given a cubicle that once had been his. When he was the star. Or as much of a star as they had there. Five by ten with a high-up window at one end. Peeling Government-Institution-Green paint. He hung up her belly dancer costume and draped the cloths for the de Milo scene on the one remaining hook. She had the boots for the opening. Here I'll help you he said but she said No. He was to go outside. He would have to help with the de Milo by putting the graffiti on her but till then no thanks. He went out and sat at the bar on a far stool. No one seemed to notice him much less recognize him. Yet it had been only six months since he had been on that very stage. It hung a foot over Charlie the tall barman's head and was generally out of reach of customers which was sometimes a very good thing. Willie was up there now flouncing about in net stockings and gloves with a garter belt that showed over his Gay 90s cincher. Fluff. Three or four at the bar watched her. No one else. In fifteen minutes Wille would be back serving drinks and encouraging the purchase of more. None of that for Juno. He sniffed and straightened his shoulders. Charlie at last saw him there and gave him a Martini & Rossi sweet vermouth. Big night said Charlie setting it down.

She'll do all right Terry said. Sure she will sure she will Charlie said Sure she will. He wiped and went back to the middle of the bar. Most booths were filled and four couples had just come in. Good: nothing worse than opening to an empty house. As the door swung back to he heard a snatch from City Sidewalks that mixed with the cacophony of the band in the corner. Fool Christmas music: should have been turned off a week and a half ago.

Then Willie got down and tried to light up but Charlie shrugged toward the booths and off she went with a tray. If she was going to smoke it would be with them. Then the band picked up again with something he'd heard a hundred times and couldn't name if he'd had to. They blared then cut and the lights went out then on again and there was Juno on the platform looking eight feet tall. With the heels she was 6'6" and the altitude exaggerated things further. The band hit it and she began to stomp. At first there was silence like Adolf Hitler at a Bar Mitzvah. Juno's face showed nothing. By God that was style. Then her act began to catch on. When her fifteen minutes were up they whistled and stamped for more. Instead they got Willie for another fifteen minutes. Then someone he didn't know but who was much the same.

The belly dance did even better and he whistled too and clapped till his hands were sore. It wasn't Boris Karloff on stage the way he had thought. She was good. At doing his stuff. Which of course he had taught her. Step by step. Although now and then there appeared something he didn't recognize and that was good too. Before she finished they began to throw money and when she finished it rained. Charlie helped him pick it up.

In the cubicle he surprised her as she was taking the ruby out of her navel and attempting to screw the gold watch in. She stopped momentarily as she saw that he saw that she had shaved. Then she went on at wedging it in. She couldn't get the stem in. Take it out he said And put the stem in first. Oh she said and tried it and found it worked. Then she began to get into her drapery and he got out the set of pencils to decorate her. He put a Sure Thing on over a phone number that would get you both the Correct Time and some advice as to which bank to do business with. He put Juno over one breast as if it were a name pin and Bruno over the other (temporarily covered) one. Across her belly he wrote Hugh Hefner is Impotent and on her backside where she couldn't see it Terry Loves Me.

It took ten minutes to get her fully graffitied and then he fastened the clips that helped hold her sheeting. You play it by ear Juno: I'm staying back here and won't be able to signal you and anyway you want to look at just one person in an audience anyway but if it seems right to you then release the clips one by one: you'll know.

He put the black stockings on her arms and sent her out. He followed a certain ways. As she climbed the ladder to the stage the black light went on and the fluorescent paint lit up then she closed the curtains and disappeared from him. They roared. He went back to her room and closed the door.

It was quiet then except for a distant drum beat and he sat and looked at the tools of what was now her trade but would never again be his. Better that way perhaps: you needed someone to guide you and she had him but he had never had anyone. Then he began to make up. Lined the brows and the lashes. Then green beneath the brows to accent his eye color. He lifted up the hair he'd brushed up on his head and let it fall down then began to stroke it with her pair of military brushes. Then he did so to the beat of the drummer keeping time for Juno: no other music came through only thump-a-thump-thump. Soon he was dancing then off came his apple green jacket. Then he kicked off his slippers. The brushes were his fans. There were three mirrors and he tried to hide himself from the reflections they showed or rather he tried to hide vital parts by turning away to the fourth wall to drop another garment. Finally he had on just his underpants and with the brushes covering his chest turned and gave the frontal mirror on the back of the door a big grind and bump just as the drummer hit the last ta-thump.

He'd timed it perfectly. Except the bump had thrown up and out his most embarrassing member and there it hung like a fob while he clutched the brushes over his scars. It was thus that Juno found him as she smashed through the door flushed and excited with triumph carrying her costume partly in front of her with one hand and the rest of it wadded around her middle. The watch was still running though perspiration ran over it and although sweat covered and blinded his own eyes he could see it was only 10:30.

She took the brushes from his hands and began to stroke his hair. You look like a Breck commercial she said. You know: the kind they put on the inside back covers of magazines. He said he knew. She stopped then and began to get dressed for her go-go bit even though she wasn't on again till midnight. She could go out of the street that way couldn't she? He said he saw no reason why not. Good she said Then you get dressed too and we'll have a snack where we went to for coffee. She lit up a Romeo y Julietta.

He thought about it.

No he said You go. Bring me back something.

Bring back what?

Oh you know—anything. She said okay and pulled on her boots. He helped her lace them while she pulled on a sweater over the lamé brassiere he had made for her. When she put on her coat he stopped her and turned her around and fumbled at her middle. She was confused till his fingers found what they were searching for and pulled out the pocket watch and set it on the dressing table. They both laughed.

After she left he opened the transom window to let out her cigar. It was too high for him to see out of without a chair and he didn't want to go to the trouble. Instead he sat looking into her mirror and then slowly began to brush his hair with one hand while concealing his chest or part of it with the other then switching quickly. A Sally Rand effect. From outside the speaker was still going on somewhere down the street playing probably to one or two or no one. By then it was We Three Kings of Orient Are and slowly he began to keep time to it.

Thinging

She lay on the bed under stark lighting in a room not especially feminine but clearly make-do. The sheet was partly off her and thrown back at mid-thigh with her shorty pajamas exposed above it. She was tummy down with her face sideways toward him where he stood in his boxer shorts looking at her blonde hair in a halo with hanks of it wet at the ends tendril-like as if she were just up from near drowning. Her eyes were closed and her breathing heavy through parted lips. Louise wearing only briefs and a tee was standing beside Jake and nudged him forward. The only sound was the low hum of the air con which was working steadily and her breath which was louder.

He knew what to do and moved closer then lifted her top a bit even though her waist already was exposed. Feeling he was acting in one of the most depraved of porn movie sets he pulled down her shorts below the inverted valentine of her butt: it was sweetly rounded at the bottom and tapered gently upward to her girlish mid-section. He was handed the box of suppositories and he removed one. When he reached down and spread her cheeks her thighs were opened enough to show the pink fig and the slot in it where of course there was no hair. Then he pushed the suppository into her rectum and felt the sphincter of her anus close around his middle finger as he did so. He withdrew his finger and quickly pulled the lower half of her pajamas up and stepped back.

Sweet butt huh?

He said nothing.

Think it's like mine Or will be?

No Louise I don't think it will be like yours. His wife's bottom was a bit wide at the top which he didn't care for but he had not married her for that any more than he supposed she had married him for his bald spot.

I think probably it's like yours or like what you would have had if you'd been female. But it's a sweet butt.

It's a sweet everything. He gave her back the box to refrigerate and said he thought he would get some alcohol to rub on her: The evaporating action will cool her down a bit. My grandmother used to do that to me and it seemed to work. Louise said she would get an ice pack for her forehead while he did so.

First he washed her hands then took the bottle from the medicine cabinet and laved her back and her butt and thighs and arms then gently lifted her and except for her face spread the alcohol on her front on tummy and the pinched nipples that when Beth was twice her present age would begin to grow. Or maybe before. When he pulled her top down he saw that his wife had been watching him with the overhead light now making a nimbus around her auburn hair. Even as he noticed that she switched the light off and told him that Doctor Harris had said her fever should break that night and then all it would take was a couple of days in bed.

Louise said She'll hate breaking her perfect record at kindergarten: she's the only one who still has one. He said he would explain it to Beth before he left for school himself. Louise led him down to the kitchen. She had the computer going: there was no space for it anywhere except in the cupboard so they kept it there. The house was small and hot with only Beth's and their bedrooms air conned: those and the bath were upstairs. Downstairs was the kitchen and what passed for a combined entry hallway a living room and a dining area. There was no basement but only a crawlspace—not big enough for a hound dog Jake had said so he put on a deck in the back where the lot fell away slightly and thus accommodated it. There was a chinaberry in the front yard and a pecan by the side which separated them though barely from the Arbuthnots. He had put a six foot magnolia in the back which meant spending more for it than they could afford. He watered the hell out of it.

When Chet his colleague at the high school had questioned the wisdom of this (since Jake and Louise surely didn't plan on staying in that house for long) he had said that the world was not a desert when he was born into it. Chet nodded but his wife Lee corrected him: Texas was. They all agreed and had gone to their card hands with the Baptist minister and his wife making two more. The latter pair had come to call and proselytize and Lee had invited them to come right in and had said they were about to have their weekly poker game and would the Reverend Doodly Pigg and his charming wife Mona care to join them? Neither broke stride and said Certainly. Nor did they comment when it became clear that neither Lee nor Chet played the game well.

Weekly session indeed. Louise later told her husband she could not for the world understand why anyone would marry a minister especially a Baptist one. He had said he guessed that some people liked to suffer and that next to marrying an alcoholic or a football coach that was the surest way to guarantee a surfeit of it.

That was only two weeks previous and at the same table where they now sat. She nudged the window more open and propped it with a one-by-one so that a sweet breeze came across the papers: not enough to ruffle them but sufficient to remind someone of a lost love in a lost town—someone whose name you had forgotten until then and the time and the place. A very silly love probably: a love of youth yet one that might have grown had things gone differently. Maybe Beth would smell something some day that recalled the high prairie wind and that would bring her back home to Arabela Texas which then could be half a world away and perhaps totally lost the way Joyce's Ireland was lost and Singer's Poland except in their tales. Her mother had once wanted to be a poet: perchance Beth would make it.

She pulled back the other kitchen chair that hadn't books on it and sat beside him: So how are we feeling about our dissertation now?

Right now we are feeling ashamed.

She nodded. He asked if that was why she wanted him to take care of Beth just then. She shook her head no. She hadn't known why at the time she had insisted and still she didn't. She shuffled the stack of papers that was her thesis. The plan was that she would submit it to San Marcos and then he would quote from it in his own work at Austin and then if he could get on somewhere she would complete her own doctorate in Anthropology and they would try for a shared appointment somewhere else or maybe wherever they then would be. As she had realized she was or would become a failed poet so had he seen the same thing about himself as a playwright.

He had read Vonnegut's remark that when he was unable to decide whether he wanted to study poetry or science he had followed the advice of his advisor to go for poetry that pretended to be science. So Vonnegut said he had majored in Anthropology. Louise had herself known an actor and writer who had sunk ten years into a play that just barely failed to make it to Broadway despite having the strong backing of his agent who was the woman who used to be Molly Goldberg on radio: he too had then opted to become an anthropologist. So would they also do.

What they came up with jointly was the notion that marriage was created to control insofar as was possible the raging sexuality of the human female.

Their reasoning was that the human male sexually did not differ significantly from any other primate but the human female did: she alone copulated face to face (at least if she wanted to) and had (sometimes) orgasms and greatly outlived her reproductive cycle and above all had no Season. The other point of the thesis was the notion that since human civilization was of comparatively recent origin that it must have come about when the human female lost her Seasonal impulses. Perhaps it came about gradually. Whichever it was surely once it came about it would be necessary to control it so that something else could get done in life. Hence marriage. With Seasonless Females the major task would be to control what otherwise would be chaos. Hence marriage as it had more of less existed until their own age. That was her poem: probably an Epic.

His play would come next and already was outlined: the intellectual establishment no longer saw much linkage between sex and reproduction and the world had moved from the Industrial Age as surely as it had abandoned the Agricultural Age and before that the Hunter-Gatherer Age. Now it was a Consumer Age: it was a Sexual Age where that was what was Consumed—Sexuality—and Pornography was its Art Form. That was his dissertation which already was approved at Austin and through it they would make their names. Pornography was itself a satire on normal sexuality so they would have to be careful not to allow themselves to be seen as satirizing a satire since a satire was a tin can tied to a dog's tail: but a satire of a satire was a tin can tied to a tin can and would not move. They agreed on that.

What we have to decide she said Is whether this thing with the Schultzes is something we want to get involved with. I have lunch with Hansen's secretary every day and she isn't sure where he stands on it except that he will be the Vicar of Bray: he will continue to be Superintendent of Schools.

She and Jake knew by heart the story Chet and Lee had told them: that when they first arrived in Arabela it was a Sunday afternoon and nothing was open and their hotel room was not ready and there was no place to eat. But Chet had seen a sign for Schultz's and thought the place might sell food and went in. It did sell food if licorice panties and bras counted but he and Lee were hungry and they went into the incongruously located porn shop: not only did Arabela look like a tableau from an artist currently residing in a rest establishment but the fact of Schultz's being there was equally strange. But they were hungry. And they saw a film after Chet signed them in under fictitious names. When they got back to the hotel to register he found his wallet missing and realized where he misplaced it: but the Schultzes—an elderly brother and sister act—claimed no one with his name had been there. They had stolen his wallet and nothing could be done about it. In it the Schultzes got the $900 Lee's parents had advanced them for their rental deposit and first month's billing. Two weeks later a group calling itself the Council for Ordinary Decency had sued to shut down the emporium. And now as Mrs. Murphy said the fight was on. And Jake had been asked to testify. Did Principal Hansen want him to? In the slightly over one year he'd known him Jake decided Hansen seemed to want what was best for Hansen.

That's our superintendent's principle he said: I know he doesn't want to parlay it into anything but just wants to maintain the status quo. The question is do we Do we really care whether a dumpy old brother and sister couple run a porn shop in Arabela Texas? The whole matter will be moot directly anyway as soon as computer porn is available in the home. Which is now.

She realized she had read her concluding chapter halfway though and didn't recall a word. She shook her head at herself but he took it to be an answer. Then what did they want?

She said she didn't mean that didn't mean no. She meant she didn't know. They weren't in a position to be out of a job at the end of the year: her degree would be in hand then but his wouldn't not for one more year anyway. He mentioned there was the possibility that perhaps they ought to have some principles.

Not very scientific she said Not very professionally anthropological. All we are to assume is that all cultures are equally valid and to observe. He nodded Sure and grimaced: neither was much a believer in their god. He said there was one thing though: Beth's. He didn't finish so his wife did: Her butt? He nodded. It was true: if all cultures were equal then the pornographic culture also was equal and so therefore was that of Pedophilia. Beth's illness had the effect of putting a human butt on pedophilia. No doubt about it: that was the supreme Eros for some and they both knew it. At least the Schultzes liked cats. Lee had said she often saw them in the Piggly Wiggly buying cat food.

He asked if he could make her some iced tea and was told that he could. When he set it before her with some fresh mint in it the way they both liked it he reseated and said that he had met with Lester Gilhooley that day and had been asked to testify for the prosecution.

Who's Gilhooley? She thought she knew everyone involved.

The man Citizens for Ordinary Decency have brought in. CfOD isn't just a local organization they're national. Like NAMBLA only in a different direction. He's the lawyer who'll try the case not the local prosecutor not Parsons.

She understood that rightly enough: against any opposition at all Parsons surely would lose. Who was the opposition? NAMBLA? Were they in it?

Maybe as a Friend of the Court if it comes to that but I think the defense would want to keep them out unless they want to lose hands down. I think it's the Mafia or some Mafia-descended group. I think that's who controls Porn. They used to be dominant in prostitution and in booze when that was illegal maybe now in drugs. Whoever it is could beat Parsons. But Gilhooley seems savvy. Chews gum with his mouth open.

She made a face but got the idea: open-mouthed mastication was just the thing in Arabela. So what have you decided? What does Mr. Milton say in Areopagitica? She had chided him often enough about his Jewish ancestry making him somehow unable to leave well enough alone: even if that ancestry was partial it always seemed to be enough. He was working on the dissertation in absentia to keep from getting into further trouble at UT.

I don't think the Latin secretary for Oliver Cromwell Lord Protestor of England and Ireland had Porn in mind. I'm going to do it. Make a fool of myself. Of you too. If you don't want me to do it though I won't. I haven't agreed yet but I want to. He did not look at her but only stared at the computer. She saw he hadn't typed a word either: no more than she had read one. She sipped her tea and nodded. Then she wiped her wet hand somewhat dry on her shorts and squeezed his hand with it. His hand was wet too and hot: You're not getting sick are you?

He said he wasn't and she squeezed his hand again. I'm with you she said: We'll do it.

You too? He looked at her with hope.

No just you. You be the fool for both of us. Same as always. But I'm with you. Whatever comes. He turned his head down and nodded. She thought his eyes were tearing and turned away then got up to check the refrigerator for anything she could.

And so that was how Jake Henry came to be duly sworn and seated. The first one he noticed after he took his place in the box was Hansen whose face showed no emotion one way or the other. Nor had Hansen offered him an opinion of any sort in the time it took things to get started. Hensen would be Vicar of Bray come High Church Low Church or Whig Hansen would be Vicar of Bray sir. Louise was there too seated next to Lorna Doone or whoever—Mona Pigg. The Schultzes were across the aisle and down.

The lawyer was everything that Gilhooley was not: tailored (Gilhooley wore a suit with stitched lapels) was tanned (pale) and urban (the gum was being chewed even then) a Californian. Which struck Jake as appropriate that someone from Ultima America would defend the Schultzes even if the man he had learned originally was from North Carolina and was the son of a Methodist minister.

Lester Gilhooley had told him that much and said Jake could offer an opinion on the worthiness of the films confiscated from the Schultzes that he'd seen since the defense witnesses had been allowed to do so: a Social Worker and a Psychiatric Nurse had both been produced who said Porn films were good and each said she used them in her work in her counseling. Lester privately had said to him that the films were ridiculous: a guy meets a girl in a gym and two minutes later they're both stripped and he was down on her. Ridiculous. Yet the MSSW and the RN recommended them. Jake supposed those two were being paid and probably handsomely. He could use some cash but none had been offered.

Charles Mallard smiled genially and asked after his credentials and was interested in his dissertation topic which Jake described elliptically as having to do with Sexuality and Civilization.

They do go together then?

He thought so: we live in a zoo in a jungle he said quoting a Peter DeVries novel (he couldn't recall which): It's the first thing that needs to be controlled.

What needs to be?

He thought of a childhood visit to the Brookfield Zoo when he visited his father in the summer and noticed the hyper-sexuality of the tightly crowded and confined monkeys where some were copulating and some masturbating. His father had smiled but Jake had been embarrassed.

What needs to be controlled? Sexuality he said. Mallard let that pass but did say that of course he had seen the selected films. He had: the two chosen by CfOD as typical—both the von Masoch / de Sade one and the one about rape.

And were you aroused?

It was a good question: if he lied and said no then there was no cause for alarm about such films.

Of course.

And his intellectual response to them?

He doubted whether the rape film was accurate: the woman hated it for roughly five seconds then was converted. As for the other only it only showed how things had changed: formerly those acts were reserved for the aristocracy and now anyone could participate—one no longer need be a marquis or a baron. Mallard liked that or pretended to. And what exactly was his literary evaluation? Or would it be anthropological?

Literary I suppose: my MA is in English. Roughly it's this: a critic spoke of flat and round characters. The flat ones are static and the round ones are capable of becoming aware of themselves. In certain sub-genres—Science Fiction and Whodunits and Horror for example— all the characters are flat. In better stuff there are some round ones. In Porn no one is round. In fact they are not even flat they are stick figures. They are Things. People who have become Things and pretend to like it that way. There is much in society that causes us to treat ourselves and others that way but we shouldn't do it.

Mallard had no further questions. Gilhooley had none at all but paused in his gum chewing to smile. Then they recessed for lunch. Chet and Lee looked busy when he went past them he supposed because they were on the other side. Mona Pigg and Louise wanted to go to the Chat 'n Chew though where the country ham was good as were the red-eye and the corn bread and beans.

Advertisements for local businesses lined the wall up near the ceiling of the café though there was ample space for more of them. Schultz's Movie's was among the few. The place damnably was air conned to the point of chilliness. Mona who was downright skinny ought to have been cold but didn't appear so. Jake didn't see why Louise and Lee envied her figure there being so very little of it. He supposed fashion designers had done a job on women: preferring boys they had chosen models who looked as much like them as possible and now women thought that was what other men liked. Oh well.

Mona doesn't agree with our thesis Louise said: She thinks marriage was devised to civilize men. Jake said there was no percentage in that theory not for them. Mona wondered if there weren't some facts involved. Somewhere at least.

Louise shook her head nope: in Social Sciences you could say what you liked so long as you had statistics to prove it. The challenge lay in creating the statistics. Like footnotes in the Humanities: there you could say anything you wanted so long as you could prove someone else said it before you: Then it's scholarship.

Louise and Jake went for the bean soup which also was good at the C & C but Mona was for the ham and red-eye. She swallowed some looked around and said she wouldn't like it to get out but her general view of Sex was that God was drunk that day. She giggled at her own joke and they did too once she signaled it was all right to do so. But really she thought women used sex to bring men to love: women made fools of themselves for love since their bodies had a so much greater stake in it than men. Men lied about everything else and made up schemes to explain the world and thereby stuff it in their socks.

We just pretend to believe the crap you all come up with. In Porn you make women into men too. Maybe the whole modern world does. Maybe your thesis is correct. Then she shrugged while they stared at her and she went on cutting up her ham still looking down. Then she said the way one might say Yeah and sows might fly And Guccione might be correct too when he says Hefner glorifies women but Flynt trashes them.

After that Louise was the first to speak: Your hair is beautiful: so full. Mona said she hated the color. It was mousy. Her eyes were large and soulful. But drab like her hair.

Jake said he had learned something interesting about the Schultzes something having to do with Chet's and Lee's telling about seeing them in Piggly Wiggly and buying so much cat food. What was interesting about that Louise asked and Mona still bent over her meat watched him with her muddy browns.

They don't own any cats.

Then they all looked down while they finished their lunch.

Poker With Wojciech

On the tram from Stegny where his grain elevator called an apartment from which he was going over to Dessault's there was a stop so abrupt that it jolted him out of his thoughts of Kitty O'Something. Her name really was O'Shaughnessy but since she really was indeed Something everyone at the American Studies Center called her that. She had gone to Denmark recently but he thought she had gone alone. Though on returning she had asked him if all Polish men were un-circumcised and he had stupidly said You're asking me? But she seemed to get over it quickly.

Felix looked for the cause of the stop and saw the driver get off and pick up someone flopped across the tracks and move him over to and against the waist-high barrier rail that separated the north-south trollies. The fellow sat there just as he was placed with his legs straight out and his head to one side. A light was over him despite it not being a regular stop and thus there being no need for one but there was one anyway: he looked like a subject for Edward Hopper had Hopper done late twentieth century Polish subjects in this example of the Intel-lectuals' Paradise. Of course late twentieth-century Poland looked a lot like early-twentieth century industrializing America so it was a fit. Also there were trams then in America. But he didn't recall Hopper ever doing drunks. And for Hopper light was everything though here the light was wrong.

It wasn't all that wrong though since artificial lights tended to be similar in all cities. It was the buildings of Warszawa that reminded him of depression-era America the tail-end of which he had caught. If he had spent more time in Chicago other than the years at the Art Institute perhaps he would have seen bullet pocks on buildings there too but probably not: in Chicago they were plastered over. Here the war had been over for forty years and the holes still were there. Even so there were scenes that were fit subjects for a Hopperesque treatment and when it turned warmer in three or four months he might try a canvas or two. If willing to risk the finished product being confiscated by Emigration Officialdom when he finally left Polska then he could photograph it now and work from those: they could claim it as a National Treasure unless he was willing to subvert their morality with what to him would be minor money.

Photographing would be all right so long as he took no shots of train stations or bridges since the Polish Milicja had rules against that. Maybe tramways too. After all they once had been militarily significant as had cavalry. The Poles seemed slow to acknowledge changes in tactics though probably the photography law was a Soviet one. A Sociologist at the University told him that there had been Jewish Colonels of Cavalry: he hadn't said anything about Polish anti-Jewishness but the fellow seemed to think it needed bringing up.

Felix took the occasion to ask if the Polish cavalry had indeed charged the Panzers and was informed that indeed they had: they were surrounded and their officers gave the troopers the choice of surrender or attack. So they hoisted and then lowered their lances and charged. They could have survived if they had surrendered Felix said Since they were not fighting Soviets in that instance. The Sociologist knew he was referring to Katyn and changed the subject. Sociology and Philosophy were the two academic areas the Marxists absolutely had to have complete control of: the one to prove their science practically and the other to prove it theoretically. So he was glad he had said it though actually only the officers would have been killed: they were leaders and more likely to be conservative. That was the operative formula and there was this male need to formulate the world and stuff it in one's socks. As a rationalization of the Road to Power. Or at least it was for those who chose to use the ideas. Those who invented the schemes were only trying to write the formula and stuff it in their socks. Auden was right when he wrote that there never was a female colossal silly on the level of Kant or Hegel. He may as well have added Marx too. But it would never end. The best America had produced was Calhoun who never became a major player on the world stage.

Then with a lurch and a clang they moved forward again with alternating pleasant sideways jerks. To his left he then suddenly saw across the small aisle that Marsden Hartley was sitting with a copy of Trybuna Ludu on his lap but Marsden was staring straight ahead. He wondered if Hartley's Prussian officer lover had died on the Eastern or Western front in the Great War. If the former then he might well have fallen in what once again had become Poland. Or maybe a part that was now the Soviet Union. But not in Warszawa: Hartley was looking in the wrong place. Anyway he would tell Kitty about it and perhaps she would be amused. But would someone who wrote and taught Lit know who Hartley was? Her area was American so maybe. His own dear Deirdre was studying literature and hoped to teach it. The older daughter and more like him. He would see her in Berlin at Christmas if she didn't leave there with friends for skiing. She had taken his side against her mother although he had not asked her to.

And then they were passing the disused ski jump that had been put up at the same time and too near to an apartment building also being put up and the different planners didn't consult each other. The result was that a potential Olympic champion overshot and went straight into the apartment wall straight into the old mieszkanie. Then though the ski jump was an obvious mistake and useless they nonetheless left it up. Next it was his stop and he got off to go up the street to Dessault's for poker. Since the connecting bus to the tram had been late so was he. He passed the street where Jaruzelski lived and turned into Dessault's and pushed open the unlocked gate. He only partially closed it behind him in case someone else was late though it wasn't likely: on the street perpendicular to Dessault's were three cars with Corps Diplomatique stickers on them. He hung on the hall tree his hat and coat—both had cost a tenth of what they would in the States—and noticed all of the other coat labels save one were Ami or Canadian. Suzy came up the steps on four game legs to sniff and bark. After she was petted she shut up and hopped down after him. Bon soir Arcite he yelled in the Cajun that Dessault liked to hear.

Arcite yelled in return to him backwards without getting up: a hand was in play. Others greeted him sideways or with short nods: two Canadians an American Colonel and a Sergeant and an Embassy man who may have been CIA and Arcite who ran the American School K-8 and who was always host since the Milicja allowed no drinking and driving. Much of Arcite's 250 pounds were from Heineken's.

Felix said that since with him there were seven he took it that once again Wojciech wasn't going to make it. Arcite shook his head with his mouth full of beer then swallowed: Phoned his regrets yesterday. Felix said he supposed that was why he got to fill in but the Colonel said no that it was he who was the seventh man: he also had never got to play with Jaruzelski. Arcite said it was just as well since the General had access to lots of złoty which also meant he could get beaucoup dollars at the unofficial rate and thus could bluff a lot of hands. Besides that one of the Canadians who was in some sort of Military Intelligence work and was sharp said Besides that he always wears his boots and he clicks his heels when he's trying to fill (which is often) and it drives you crazy.

Everyone agreed with that evaluation as he bought five dollars' worth after the third card in seven card stud. They allowed no wild card games and played too much 727 but it was at least human contact. The other Fulbrighters were married and the Poles at Akademia were married and he had not found the Polish women climbing all over him as he had been warned jokingly that they would be. He was too old. A few very young and very bright and very pretty women had smiled a lot but they were much too young: they wanted the blue and gold document in his hip pocket and he couldn't blame them but they were much too young.

The only woman he saw regularly was Dorota who cooked for him thrice weekly and shopped and stocked the larder and did laundry all for $50 per month paid in zielony though not in złoty: green not gold.

Polish money more or less was papier toaletowy. Except that real toilet paper could not be had easily save when a shipment came in to some Paper Store unannounced. For that reason one carried in a pocket a length of string sufficiently long to run ten rolls—the allotment—on a necklace at which no one laughed but rather asked excitedly where it was bought before hurriedly running off to join what they hoped would be a fruitful wait in line. Dorota found him toilet paper indeed maybe sold it off her own necklace. Why there was a shortage he could not figure. Possible they needed the paper for the Party newspapers which also did admirably for wiping if you didn't mind printer's ink on your butt. Arcite had told him the Poles preferred it that way since they then could make love and read at the same time.

Over the play of the evening Felix won $18 which was about the average monthly wage for a Pole. No wonder the pretty young women smiled and Dorota had been willing to follow him to the grain elevators of Stegny (which when he was in a bad mood he called Smegma) when he was moved from his first assigned apartment near Old Town after the SB apparently decided he was not a spy. Dorota had to travel across town to do so but it was fantastic money. Probably the second place wasn't wired though surely the nice one near Old Town was and it even had a telephone in it though one had to get on the list to make a long distance call since a censor had to be ready to listen. It could take a day. But they had decided he was only an Art Prof. So he had been moved to a high-rise that looked like a prairie grain elevator. All the socialist countries he had seen had them though in America the most the Progressive Social Planners could do was foist them on to the poor. When he showed a film that included the imploding of Pruitt-Igoe the class was silent and still in shock when they left the room.

The next day at the American Studies Center he set it up to lecture on Hopper since all American visiting profs were required to give one speech or two on something. He had thought there might be interest on her part when Kitty O'Something had asked him to go with her party to Powązki Cemetery on All Saints': it was an odd cemetery in that they honored artists as national heroes. And the dead at Katyn.

Kitty was red haired and green eyed with batteries always fully charged. He liked that in a woman since he always had struck himself and seemed to strike others as being about a quart low. The secretaries pretended to like her but didn't because of the luck of her draw in being American: they too were trim and well dressed. God knew how they managed that. Their only failing showed in the Polish inability to make colors fast: socks had to be washed separately unless one wanted them all grey. But worse was the reddish purple hair that many local young women had: he was sure they weren't trying for it but that it came from the same inept chemistry. Anyway Kitty was naturally red (he thought) and even if he wasn't she at least was perpetually fully charged.

The dislike of the secretaries did not disqualify her for him however. The secretaries all had MAs as did the librarians and were smart and maybe worked for the SB or at least had to report to it. No matter: on him there was nothing to report. He wasn't even having an affair with Kitty who though still married said she was divorcing. She was a sort easily recognized (especially by women) as the one who always had first choice among whatever group of men she happened to be in. Like most such women she had no children.

She was joking even then in the central office with a Pole with a clown's face almost like Jaruzelski's apple cheeks and fat upper lip and frizzed hair on the sides with none on top. That was Jerzy Something. Felix was happy to have kept his own hair in full thickness although it had silvered: Jerzy's was the color of the inside upper end of the tail of the horse he rode on the farm in South Dakota when the Jensens took him in. They were dead twenty years and he'd never properly thanked them though he had mentioned them at Święta Anna on Sundays: prayers for the dead. Often a military band and two companies of goose stepping infantry would pass by while mass was in session. Their music and slapping boots penetrated the church. On the walls were medals won by an earlier generation of Polish soldiers who saw no conflict in dedicating them to a saint nor did the church mind posting them. It was so also in the church near the castle is Kraków where they had gone while being on two weeks of orientation for newcomers. There the guide had told them almost as many Poles had been killed by Poles themselves since the War as the Germans and Soviets had killed during the War. He meant abortion. He was surprised so few of the Americans dipped their fingers in the holy water on entering and exiting. At an Old Town church in Warszawa there were saints in every other colored glass window with Polish heroes in the alternating ones. Once Kitty had gone there with him.

He told Kitty he'd seen Marsden Hartley the night previous and Jerzy spoke quickly to indicate he did not appreciate the interruption: he had himself seen Wallace Stevens and Robert Frost on the same train from Kraków within a fortnight and though they were in the same compartment they ignored each other. He like Kitty taught American Literature. Kitty said she had seen Gertrude Stein that very morning at Plac Zamkowy standing there at parade rest with her all-wooden umbrella. Jerzy pursed his lips as well as one with a fat overlip could and wondered if Alice B. Toklas was inside doing some shopping for them. Was there with her a woman with a small neat waxed moustache?

Kitty assured Jerzy that there was.

Aha! Then you saw the both of them! He turned his back somewhat and poured hot water into a glass with tea leaves in it then put it down and poured a second one. How they could hold a thin glass filled with hot water Felix could not understand and always put his in a wicker holder. Jerzy gave the first to Kitty and kept the second himself. Kitty too partly turned a shoulder from him and toward Jerzy and said that though she wasn't quite sure but was still pretty sure she had seen—guess who?—working at Bank Handlowy. Jerzy shrugged and she sparkled her eyes at Felix for a moment to include him. He didn't know either.

T. S. she emphasized and then added quietly Eliot.

Jerzy whistled.

It seems all our important figures come here after they die he told Jerzy But where do the famous Poles go?

They all died in exile! He laughed and the two other Poles seated near the secretary's desk did too. He thought probably all the Poles there would like to live and die in exile or at least go West for a couple of years to earn and save money. He laughed too and took out a twenty-four cent Romeo y Julietta after offering them around from his case and getting an acceptance from one of the men—Andrzj—who were sitting and talking with Beata. Andrzj said he'd wait to light it till he was outside and Felix announced he was going for a walk. He'd used his last match from a U.S. embassy book and he discarded it on a table after writing inside it a commentary about the irregularity of Gorbachev's sex life. Beata immediately picked it up and laughing passed it around to others who also laughed to include Jerzy and finally Kitty who took Jerzy's hand and said she'd walk too. Nothing otherwise seemed to pass between them.

Andrzj wasn't a bad fellow in fact could be quite bitingly witty: when a visiting American sociologist gave his obligatory talk and of course did it on his dissertation the American said that the USA had not desegregated on moral grounds but had done so solely because of King's and others' boycotts. The Polish students were quite good and sat glumly when the American asked for commentary and then Andrzj said he saw that the fellow was a Market-Place Man. The Sociologist looked as though someone had accused him of being religious and wondered how Andrzj had got that. But the students had got it: Oh said one of them I wish Poles were as free as American Blacks were in 1950.

It took a while to instruct the sociologist that boycotts didn't work in Socialist countries even if the boycotters were not rudely dispersed. But Andrzj was not the one Kitty was interested in.

She would walk too she said.

Then she turned to him and said That is if it's all right with Felix.

Of course it was all right. Andrzj lit their cigars and they walked and puffed behind the pair who went on comparing the literary sorts they had seen in Poland. Andrzj had been to America and yet had come back: strange. Since Old Town was visible to him and Felix knew it had been rebuilt from old plans after the War he asked if Andrzj had seen the American version of Old Town which we called Disneyworld. Andrzj said it wasn't at all the same since though they had indeed rebuilt their

Old Town after it was flattened after the War but it was not a matter of creating a child's version of history but rather the Poles' refusal to be robbed of theirs. Point taken. But yes he had seen it. He shuddered a little.

Then Felix had an idea: How about if we go to the Hotel Victoria for lunch and then go out to the green where the ghetto once was and see if Isaac Bashevis Singer is hanging out there? The men shook their heads and said they had other plans. At Nowy Świat they went one way and he and O'Something moved toward the Victoria but settled on the Europejski instead since it was closer. He asked if he had scared them off because for them it would be expensive: I would have paid for everyone.

She knew. And they knew. But there was somewhere they had to go. Then she saw something in an empty leather shop and took his arm and led him toward it. He didn't want to go in with a lit cigar and held back but decided to Kennedy it in his pocket and risk burning a hole but at least his other arm would be held by Kitty. As soon as they got in she decided there wasn't anything she wanted there anyway but five more people had queued behind them: the shop must have had something suddenly available! But when the two of them left so did the others: false alarm.

Obiad was the main meal in Poland and began about one so they were a minute or two early but were let in. They got seats not too near the dance floor which was unoccupied at that hour anyway. The last time he was there was at night when there was a band and a Pole in a sleazy brown suit had escorted his lady to the hardwood center then kissed her hand before they began to twirl. Downstairs was a more intime bar which even had a strip show if a young woman quickly taking off the top half of her costume counted as such. That was the first half. An hour later the second half involved her dropping everything at once and then fleeing as the lights went out momentarily.

Their waiter bent forward and quietly asked if he wanted to change money but he had plenty and said no. They ordered everything and still the bill would be only three dollars or so each unless they got vodka and even it would add little. The one thing Communist Poland never ran out of. But they made do with herbata though he thought perhaps of their excellent juice called sok: Kitty said she had got used to their tea and liked it rather. She had to be careful not to gain weigh as most American women did in Warsaw because of the good pastry: men lost (Felix had lost thirty pounds) but women gained. O'Something turned the talk back to Singer: was he really American if he wrote in Yiddish? Felix thought it wasn't the Yiddish that disqualified him but his long beginnings in central Europe: Eliot was American wasn't he and Auden English? She supposed so. But she wasn't sure she liked Singer: his Lublin world is gone. The war ended it.

Felix said everyone's world was gone with the war even as it would have been without the war but more slowly: for three million Polish Jews and three million Polish gentiles the world ended totally. But it was what wars did: a colleague had told him that the irony of war is that it's fought to preserve the status quo and nothing more surely changes it. Even as the irony of revolution is that it is done to change things and mainly it changes the names: she'd told him that was why History courses were bracketed by wars. What artists do is preserve what otherwise would be lost without them. And to show us how poignant it was. And sometimes beautiful.

What area is your colleague in?

History. Sort of like me: I paint but don't teach painting. She wondered why and he said he wasn't good enough or maybe wasn't neurotic enough so he got a PhD: there was more or a break in Art between painters and historians than there was in English between writers and critics. Kitty's eyes fixed him with that one: Critics hate us! The only reason I can teach both Literature and Imaginative Writing is that I'm at a small campus. But she insisted the critics there too were at the least made uncomfortable by the writers.

Because they depend on your sort for a livelihood but know if what-his-name—Stevens—did sit on the train he'd rather talk to you than a critic? Exactly she said but added he might prefer to talk to another insurance man: he kept his lives separate until after the fourth martini and then they got slurred.

Felix wondered whose didn't.

She smiled then said You know I had a reason for arranging this obiad between us. He was pleased to hear it but hoped his expression didn't change nor that he reddened. He thought maybe the Irish law firm of Muldoon Fagan and Muldoon had perked up a bit but there was a table cloth hiding them so it mattered little. One thing she said Is that there ought to be a Christmas party for the Polish staff and for us and I have a nice and centrally located place and I wonder if you would care to co-host it with me. Smegma where he lived was too far. He said he would and maybe they should have eggnog: he thought the Poles would like it. She said the Poles would like anything alcoholic. Could he also bring a carton or two of American cigarettes from the Pewex to put packs from around and about on the tables and such He could and he would get the bourbon there: Jim Beam was not five dollars a fifth. Ah the Pewex where one could buy anything for western money but nothing for Polish: As the little Polish woman said on coming back from visiting relatives in Chicagu it was just like Warszawa where you could buy anything for American money just like in Warszawa. And you could buy nothing there with Polish money just like in Warszawa.

He thought she was only pretending not to have heard that one but quickly went on to the second item: she had a deck of playing card she'd brought back from her long weekend trip to Copenhagen and he might want to use them at his next game. She knew he loved poker. He accepted the gift and quickly learned they were obscene. He pocketed them while someone at the next table observed: obscene cards wouldn't matter but other things might. It pleased him that he was perhaps suspected of doing something subversive of the Polish People's Republic. The law firm was again clearing its throat and he told them to be quiet and to speak only when called to the bar. If men tried to formulate the world and lied to themselves and confounded and terrified the world by their need to stuff the formula in their socks then women lied to themselves about love and did themselves in that way. Still it was better than what men did. Though the Rosa Luxemburg Light Bulb

131

Factory which was visible from Kitty's apartment was named for a horrible woman who more than pretended to believe the foolishness of men's theories: Aquinas however had noted that the occasional aberration did not disprove the general rule. He hoped Thomas was correct. The law-men were quiet and waited their call which did not come.

Whatever might be pled later on by Muldoon and Company it was clear Kitty had nothing on the docket for that afternoon and left him after lunch. But Jerzy caught him at the Center and quietly invited him in to the conference room and offered him a glass of tea. He asked if Jerzy wasn't having any and was shown where a glass was already sitting. So it was planned. Jerzy rather delicately looked around and then said he would like to talk to him elsewhere about something literary he could perhaps help him on. As he said that he looked up at what were supposed to be water pipes. Felix nodded and agreed to see him at the Europejski Hotel for coffee at ten the next morning. Since Jerzy's father was a career diplomat they would have to be careful.

Kitty having removed herself from the equation he went past the one synagogue which was identified as such by a face cut into the cement wall of a fellow who looked like Henry VIII with an even funnier hat on then on to the Wielke to see the opera which happened to be Abduction From the Seraglio in a theatre that seemed to be trying to create the impression that the scrim was a moonscape: not his favorite Mozart but for a forty cent ticket he got a second row seat and got to see eunuchs in Close Order Drill roller skate onto the stage while knitting. They each wore magenta bloused trousers with a gold stomacher and a green bolero jacket: the State did spend for Art no doubt about it. In the lobby there were six different busts of Ernest Hemingway of which a couple looked like him and there was one of Josef Tadeusz Konrad Korzienowski. Odd but for forty cents who cared?

What was said the next day was that Jerzy began with asking him what one called the Polish National synmphony after its triumphal tour of the West. Felix didn't know. A String Quartet said Jerzy. Then he told Felix he had found his capital getting low and he wondered if Felix knew anyone at the American embassy who help him with that. Suspecting a set-up he became nonchalant and said he might know someone who played poker who would know someone though he wasn't sure of it. Jerzy was satisfied with that.

All around them were people of whom any number could have been Jerzy's handlers. But Felix said okay. Back on Nowy Świat was an array of yellow and white papal flags somehow placed there because of Jan Pawel Drugi. But no goose stepping infantry with a band. That night at the game (which again Wojciech was unable to attend) he mentioned it to the embassy man and Arcite immediately looked up at the water pipes circling the room and suggested they might want to talk about that outside. So at the break they did. The fellow said he wasn't in the business himself but he thought he knew someone who was and he would pass the information along although he doubted whether Jerzy would "have the stuff." But okay. Sure.

Then he broke out the cards and they played one round but it was not successful since they were betting on what was pictured on the cards rather than what their value was at poker: Arcite had claimed victory with a full house (three group orgies and two cornholers) but the Canadian Sergeant said no that he had four fellatios. Actually neither really had anything worth betting on so they left the money in the pot and gave him back the dirty cards and returned to the regular deck. He did ask the embassy man why he Felix would himself be someone Jerzy would ask to do that for him and was told perhaps to check him and perhaps indeed to raise some money. The fellow smiled and observed that surely Felix would have to admit that his cover was better than that of the embassy man. He agreed.

The next day he quickly drew the party invitations one by one on eight by eleven school paper he folded into quarters: on the front of each one were what he thought to be amusing faces that started with a circle that led to a downward loop that came back up into a circle parallel to the other one. Then he added eyebrows and moustaches and so on that made each one different. Kitty liked them. A Pole who also was an artist laughed at them: they were all penises he said. Felix looked again and realized the fellow was right. But only if one was looking for such. But as everyone knew artists were in fact looking. Deirdre had said as much of him too though he doubted it. Of course Dahlberg had said O'Keefe's flowers were all vaginas.

He wanted to tell Deirdre of Kitty but had no phone since it cost a $1000 bribe to the fellow in charge of the unit that installed them so he went to the Hotel Victoria. Writing her would be three weeks getting the few hundred miles to her since the police would read it and then three more weeks for a reply for the same reason. But the hotel had phones and he could stay for the Polish rate and could pay in złoty: at the unofficial rate it came to around eight dollars for what they claimed was a five star hotel and really was worth four. Breakfast was included. He petitioned for a line as soon as he got there and then read some Erich Heller until he heard Deirdre's voice six hours later. She would indeed be absent from Berlin at Christmas but perhaps they could meet at semester break. He agreed and told her about Kitty: what did she think the lady was up to?

Deirdre thought Kitty was up to him and that he should go for it. He told her he was fortunate to have such a daughter and she laughed with him and said she liked him too.

He went to the sauna and then had a long hot bath and slept until breakfast which was ample and rather western. The only thing wrong was the German commercial traveler smoking a cigar next to him at the counter. He tried hard to feel good about Germans but every time he got to doing so he met some more of them. He walked for a bit in the Victory Park opposite the hotel where the not-too-bad colossal monument to victory was and where the ghetto had been. At the base of the park was another memorial consisting of a rather good conglomerate casting of Polish Jews all of whom were naked. Without climbing on the thing he couldn't be sure but it appeared they were not circumcised though the sculptor was Jewish.

When he later rode the trolley and then the bus to Kitty's with his bag of bourbon cigarettes Courvoisier and candies he saw Warszawa as not so bad a town: true it was grey with little commercial advertising (why should there be anything when the State controlled what was made and sold?) and police everywhere and there were grain elevators where people lived and indeed he was going to one now though higher-ups in the Party had very nice places indeed on nice streets indeed. But that was so almost everywhere and every place had its social difficulties. Soon he would see Kitty.

Who was not ready when he got there but finished dressing in her open-doored bedroom and came out scented nicely with a perfume he didn't recognize. She wondered if he liked her dress.

He did. Cost eight dollars she said: Would have been ten times that at home.

He nodded approval and began mixing as soon as she gave him the bowl. She had nutmeg but no kremówka. What was that? Cream for whipping. To float on top of the eggnog.

So they went out and found some fairly easily. Dairy products one could get and vegetables that grew in sandy soil. She held his arm while they walked and sometimes bumped her hip against him as she strode. He knew what that meant. She spoke also of how excellent her Amer Lit students were though she had heard the English Linguists were top of the line: it was the best ticket out of Poland. Education she said was the bottom but he corrected her: the Poles termed Education as Pedagogy but he had been told the Catechism major was worse and that it was how you got into the university if you couldn't do it any other way. There one was taught the Gospel according to Marx and Ulyanov and became a teacher of it somewhere. Maybe in the Army: Jaruzelski had been a Political Officer in the Soviet-controlled portion of the Polish Army. It was the worst. She said she supposed so but stopped bumping into him on the way back.

Then people began coming. Several brought gifts of flowers and one waxy item with a long yellow tongue sticking out of a red mouth was for him. He and the giver both laughed at that. He and Kitty worked different parts of the room during the party but when he caught her eye she smiled. He heard Jerzy say to another already drunk Pole that Americans were Jejeune Sentimental Romantic Naive and several things more he couldn't pick up over the din. The smoke became as thick as the crowd and the invited all seemed to be having a splendid time. Two of the women had red-purple hair. One fellow who had no hair at all introduced himself as a Philosopher. He said his only job was to write two Scientific papers a year. He did not teach but got a modest stipend. He managed to eke things out by going to France every summer for six weeks to Pick Wine. From that he saved enough to live on until the next summer.

You mean pick grapes. Yes he said To pick wine. He said his name and Felix said he knew someone of that name in America: a sometimes colleague.

Jewish?

Well he's not anything else.

The wine picker said so was he: he had survived the War by being taken in by a Catholic family who passed him off as one of their own. And now he was a Philosopher who wrote two Scientific papers a year. Felix knew what Scientific meant. A Pole he didn't know but was a friend of a docent had flown with the RAF in World War Two and only then had returned to Poland from America: he lived in San Francisco and said the Chinese were taking over. He had heard the philosopher and said most Poles had some Jewish blood because Jews had been the merchant class and had hired gentile girls to work in their homes and though Jewish girls were forbidden to their sons gentile ones weren't and often they went home pregnant and so most Poles got some Jewish blood that way.

The din was intense and wasn't helped when someone put a record on Kitty's player that had versions of limericks with Aiy Yai Yai Yai on it only with spacers he hadn't heard: Your mother swims after troop ships was one and Your mother douches anchovy was another. It was a linguist who had brought it. The man wanted him to pronounce the American car by GM that started with a P. He said Pontiac and the linguist said no that Americans dropped the tee in the name. He had asked every American there and they all kept in the tee: he had studied and taught in America and was getting frustrated by what he was hearing.

He was told again of the crew of a Polish ship in Canadian waters defecting at the time of Jaruzelski's crackdown and of a replacement crew being flown over: from cook to captain they also defected as did the airliner's crew. So they cut their losses and tried no more. The logo of Polish Airlines was an elephant.

And thus it went until the thrice-filled bowl finally was empty and the other bottles as well and the cigarette packs gone from the tables and the hors d'oeuvres made by Kitty long vanished. Almost at once the people left. He held back till there was no one left but Kitty. She smiled a bit wearily at him. Then he noticed through her bedroom door that there was a pair of feet hanging over the bed and that shoes were being dropped off them. He moved a little and saw that it was Jerzy.

Felix was sure his face was not blank this time and perhaps pale instead of flushed. As for Kitty she smiled and bade him good night with many thanks for his help but he was gone before she was through saying it all. Outside it was suddenly cold and a small grainy snow was falling which if snow can be ugly surely was the ugliest kind of snow. And just outside the door was one of the party-goers who had found his legs temporarily useless. Felix got him up and into a cab and said he'd give the fellow a ride home which at one dollar to anywhere in the city was not really a great gift. Perhaps since the fellow lived north and he lived south he would give the driver two dollars green which would be plenty.

The fellow didn't seem particularly grateful but only spoke how he too had been an artist like Felix and probably just as good but now he was terminated by the SB of the KGB from the art school and indeed was forbidden to buy paints from the government stores which of course were the only ones. He looked over with bloodshot eyes and said the only useful thing that came of it was they didn't draft artists: there was no work for an artist in the Army though they did take musicians for the bands so it wasn't just because they were more trouble than they were worth. But perhaps he shouldn't be saying this to Felix since perhaps Felix was himself KGB.

Felix was looking at the extremely ugly city that lived under stupid rules made by stupid men.

It was so ugly that not Burchfield nor any of the Ash Can School would have touched it. He looked over at the fellow whose eyes looked like oysters on the half shell. Not that he had seen any in Warsaw.

No he said I am CIA. The fellow shrugged and sagged into himself and soon was sleeping. One thing about Poland: no mean drunks. He and the driver helped the fellow to the door of his mieszkanie and then began the ride south to Smegma.

How God Covers His Mistakes

Clive had been friendly with Pamina and had begun helping with her rent for the two months or so he had been back from Malaysia before he realized that she was not always playing a hard candy around on her tongue while she spoke but rather that she only talked that way. It had irritated the hell out of him that she always had the candy rolling around there though he had been relieved that at least she didn't crunch them. Now he knew why: no candy.

When she wasn't rolling it around or seeming to as she at present was not doing she sucked it. Or seemed to suck a candy that wasn't there. She was looking off over her left shoulder the way most women and some men do: without turning the head. Her eyes were large and showed a lot of white despite her bright green irises which also were large. She had thick black lashes and eyebrows and wore the hair on her head slicked down and back like a flapper. His own eyes were piggish and getting more so with age. What hair he had left he brushed straight back as he had always done but now it splayed to either side like small bones from a well-filleted fish. What did she see?

Tha girl oveh theh. Red hed. Ah knew huh when she wah a blon.

He turned his head and saw a woman under a Raggedy Ann mop that appeared completely her own: combed back in front so it wasn't a wig. Since taking up with a younger woman he had investigated several hair replacement methods but they all failed him at the leading edge: he wasn't the sort to cowlick it and none that went straight back appeared natural.

Know her long?

139

Sin she wah knee hah to a grahoppuh an Ah wah too. Clahv—she touched hand with her fingers long and cool and clean-wiped of the barbecue ribs they'd shared a plate of (it was by the ribs he'd learned she wasn't really sucking a candy) and then said nothing as was most often her wont. He took it as her way of holding his hand. Probably a pleasant ruse she'd worked on and developed as a teenager. She wouldn't tell him her job but only said she was a Professional Illusionist: Everything she said Is illusion. Because that is so we ought to make our illusions the best we can: people live work and die for illusions. She said she was good at them.

He told her that the lumber he bought world-wide and sold locally was quite tangible. Had he always done lumber? No he did Literature in college and then a year of law school before quitting and then taught at a prep school for a year before switching to business. She asked if he regretted it.

Business instead of Literature? No he did not regret it: because of his business his children could afford prep school and good colleges. Pamina said no she meant did he regret quitting law school. He said he didn't: he had gone to law school to find out for himself whether the subject though man-made still generally was agreed upon because man was everywhere the same and hence his laws were (that is mores codified over time) or was it divinely given and with a capital L (but everywhere about the same since the deity was everywhere the same). He decided it came to the same thing and thus had answered his question so he quit. Also the writing was bad.

He said at present his business was in Malaysia which had a Very Good Climate for Business: Labor Unions (except company-run ones) were not allowed and labor was cheap and the ruling party owned the TV stations and newspapers or most of them and the Minister of the Interior could close down the rest. Since the Prime Minister was also the Minister of the Interior it was a stable country with a Good Climate for Business. She accepted that then smiled and shrugged. Then he nodded toward Raggedy Ann: What's her name?

Who Oh huh: Pamina.

But that's your name. Did her parents like Mozart too She looked blankly at him. You said your parents liked Die Zauber Flote indeed liked it so much they named you for the Queen of the Night.

Oh she said and shrugged.

Pamina fits you—black hair and all. But it seems inappropriate on a red head.

Ustah be a blon.

He wondered if Pamina had ever been a blonde and decided no that her brows and lashes were too black. Thus he was surprised when he went to meet her at their next appointment (Pamina did not like the word date) and was met by a feathered blonde who bubbled and told him to come in for a sec while she got her raincoat. She flounced ahead of him and he looked about for the slinky Pam who walked as carefully as a cat. She wasn't there. But a martini was. Not that Pam ever fixed him one but she knew it was his drink. The furniture except for having on it a new trim of what was it—organdy?—was vaguely familiar and the cheerleader-plus-ten-years was lively but where was Pam He asked.

Who? Oh Pam—she's not here. Anymore. I'm Sherry. She handed him the cold cone of a glass with three of her long and pink-tipped fingers pinching it to her thumb. She said she was having a Gibson herself.

Same thing he said. He stood awkwardly until Sherry took his arm and hipped him along to the couch: Not quite she said and wrinkled her nose. Her eyes were deep della Robbia blue. Drink up she said: It's my birthday. I'm a Virgo you know. He said he'd been one too but it was a long time ago. Sherry winked and clinked his glass and pleasantly took his arm.

So tell me about Pam: what happened to her Where'd she go?

Gone that's all. Went to where she came from. Never-Never Land I guess. She shrugged. She sounded like Iowa. Pam was from Charleston.

He recalled that Pam had been a Taurus thus the exact opposite of his Scorpio. Sherry nodded and said they should get along better than he did with Pam since their signs fit better.

I wasn't aware of not getting along with Pam though maybe I didn't since she's gone with no word of farewell.

She squeezed his hand: It wasn't that way at all. Her time was up that's all. Don't you like me better I do.

Well yes she was fine. But did she also like older men?

Sure. But not too old. She thought a moment and said You'll do. She tipped up her Gibson and batted the onion with her tongue before tapping the base of the glass and bringing the pearl into her mouth then back to her pursed lips from which she offered it to him. He took it and got his own olive for her and offered it with the nut side out but she shook her head: Don't like olives.

There was a life-sized ceramic black and white cat to his right that he'd never seen before and he offered it to the cat which also apparently did not like olives. He ate it himself.

That's Busterfer she said: He doesn't like olives either.

So I see. Had him long?

She seemed not to know what to say: Oh well he's been with me a while—comes and goes. Do you like him?

Just the right sort of cat to have.

She reached down to her side of the couch and brought up for his inspection a ceramic litter box filled with clean ceramic litter. Then she resettled it. Want to go dancing she asked with her bottom raised to him as she replaced the litter box. Something about the acoustics made her voice seem to come from the end nearer him. He bent forward and said Sure to it just as she righted herself and looked peculiarly at him then smiled.

But tell me first: were you ever a brunette.

In a previous incarnation.

Did she believe in reincarnation?

Oh yes: all the time. Whenever life gets boring. Then you begin to forget it's all an illusion and it's time to be reborn.

You sound like an Evangelical.

She didn't get it so she shook it off and hopped up and took his hand and pulled him after her.

They went to a place where the kinetic fare was mainly Petit rather than Grand Mal. He didn't recall ever dancing with Pam who preferred theatre and a late dinner. He was glad though it was the Minor Seizure sort of dance that Sherry favored though it occurred to him that it was possible that she was only breaking him in gently.

When they left it was raining slightly but he left his coat off because he was sweated. Sherry put hers on: she preferred to go straight home yes. Different from Pam. He said so. She asked what had he expected The same person? No but you do share a generational attitude: the dance style is different from mine. He'd read that when cultures changed because of technology or wars or whatever then so did their dances. Especially after wars invalidated the old ways. You'll see he said When you're no longer young and things have changed.

Maybe they won't change.

True: sometimes they stay unchanged for awhile. But comes a war or a depression or a new technology....

Sherry only shrugged.

People in my day didn't know or care much about birth signs you know. When I was young I mean. There were still traditional religions then which even if we didn't believe in them we pretended to.

We're more honest.

Birth signs are more honest? A different sort of lies he said and tuned on to the expressway that ran through what once had been a fairly nice neighborhood before it had been sawed in half. Unlike the magician's assistant it was not able to be put back together. Both the legs and the upper torso looked about as good as a disassembled dummy left out overnight in a shop window.

I think she said at last That when half-gods go whole gods come. Her smile in the slice of street light that caught it was disembodied. Something by a 1950s painter. Or a little later. He couldn't think who.

The half-god thing is Emerson isn't it? She said she guessed so. He was convinced that when half-gods left then the quarter-gods came. But he said nothing.

At her apartments she hesitated before asking him in: first date after all. Then she smiled and swept him along. She was like Pam and she wasn't. And truly blonde though he recalled that all hair could be dyed. It just couldn't be grown where there was none left.

He asked as much of the woman fussing over him in the P J Hilton. She had brought him tea which he asked for hot since it was cool inside though out of the air con Petaling Jaya was humid. Already she had washed his scalp as clean as ever it had been then took twenty minutes to do five worth of clipping. Now her fingertips sparked along his shoulders neck and scalp. Ah no she said stretching the negative out gently the way Latins also do Sexy men lose hair: good thing for man to lose hair. He returned her smile and enjoyed the rub. She was obviously Malay of the Bumiputra sort and not Chinese Malaysian or Indian Malaysian. The Chinese could fool you on that: just the day before he was walking behind one who was in jeans and he had been reminded of Pam and her stride. Or was it Sherry? Pam. It was Pam. Malaysian women of the Bumiputra sort favored what their men smilingly called the Cat Walk. The men would slide their open palms together up and down to clarify what they meant.

You here on business?

Yes. Wood business. He knew that the word Business gave him status: the death by murder of an MD had been widely reported in the press the day before but by it was meant Managing Director. Their physicians had the equivalent of the British MB but lacked the status of business people.

Your wife here too?

No. No wife. She smiled again and dug her thumbs into him. No worry about hair: no problem.

He remembered seeing ALF in reruns on his last trip. All Malays knew No Problem. Maybe it was earlier than ALF.

You're a Muslim?

Yes. She dragged that out too: All Malays Muslim. No choice unless part Portuguese. You believe Issa?

He said he supposed he did. It was a better response than any other he could think of. She smiled and dug less deeply.

When he looked presentable he waited in the lobby for the

company car to take him to the plane to fly them to the logging site. There was a Malay on the Board but only because he had sold his name to the Chinese who ran the company. The government required at least as much. The only Malays he saw were Polis (which included an occasional Sikh) around the office which was farther from the logging site than it had been before: less and less jungle. That was fine for the government which wanted the land for rubber trees anyway. Or for palm oil. He saw small palms ranged like sticks every few feet. So it was destined to become a palm oil plantation. No profit regrowing a jungle. And why not? Should only the First World enjoy the First World goodies? Or was it for them as it was with aristocratic Englishwoman of old who sniffed when she discovered that the lower orders enjoyed sex too: much too good for them.

It was true of course that such plantations led to water run-off and there were now droughts and shortages in a country with eighty to one hundred inches of rain a year: jungles soaked it up but who wanted jungles? People who didn't live in them wanted them for other people to live in. You could be in a jungle for fifteen minutes after the rain started before you felt the first drop trickle down. But the government wanted the money and he wanted the money and that was that.

A chemical plant was now nearby and putting an orange plume of some oxide nearly straight up: rain was their pollution control. But the wood was very good and it was cheap. He bought fine silk batik for Sherry in pale colors to go with her fair complexion.

When he got back Sherry was not there: Fatima was and she wasn't expecting him though on learning he was lately returned from an offi-cially Muslim country he was invited in. She wore what he guessed approximated native dress in tan and black and over it quite a lot of gold all of which went well with her olive skin black hair and eyes.

He offered her the material he'd brought Sherry which was accepted on the off-chance that she returned though clearly that was doubted. Fatima acknowledged it as very fine indeed. She set it on the oriental divan next to her and offered him a place at table with halal food that seemed to him more Pakistani or North Indian as Fatima said she was. His name?

Clive. I've never cared for it. Call me what you will.

Ala'din she said and moved to a rattan table the batik which she set next to a copy of The Place of Women in India. She made him a space next to her on the divan. He said he knew of a restaurant named Ala'din in PJ or KL (he forgot which) that offered fare such as she was serving.

And did he like it? Oh yes: very much.

Good. She wanted to know of the country he had just returned from: was it modern? Yes in the cities. Had he seen the new Blue Mosque of the East she had heard of? Yes he had in Shah Alam and indeed on returning to PJ from there on the federal Highway had found his and all other cars curbed by the Polis-escorted motorcade of the Sultan of Selangor so that the Sultan might pass in unimpeded majesty.

And did the women dress modestly? Yes by American standards save the Chinese who might wear anything. She was pleased. Next to her was a ceramic replica of an all-black cat he remembered from art books: the sort Egyptians were said to worship.

When dinner was over and plates gathered (she refused to let him help) she returned with a Tarot deck. He asked did Muslims believe in divination?

It is from Egypt you know that the Tarot came. Originally it was for telling the tides of the Nile. Do you want to be read? He supposed so.

She saw that he was the King of Hearts and that behind him was much travel and uncertainty—and a marriage long ago?

Yes: long ago. Two children: grown.

She nodded and said the Knave was him as a young man. All young men look like that she said: Supercilious self-pleased and also uncertain. She told him his travelling was nearly at an end with a career change soon before him. His prosperity would continue and there was before him one last journey and then a bride from India. He doubted whether he would ever again go to India.

I did not say you would. Look: here is the World. It has all four Gospel beasts on it. And beside it The Wheel of Fortune! Her brows lifted into sable crescents and he thought he saw that she wore contacts.

The same four beasts are in it and together it can only mean very good fortune indeed.

Indeed. I had thought of an early retirement.

That soon will be possible she said and gathered the cards in a lavender veil before replacing them in a small jeweled casket. She seemed to have come to the end of something but he didn't know what. So he stood and he carefully took her right hand into his and kissed the fingers. No traditional Arab woman would have been pleased by such an act but (nor would one have been alone with him) but she smiled broadly: perhaps he would like to call again? He would.

But he didn't. Not until for a birthday treat for himself did he find her and that when he chose to go to lunch at what once was the best downtown place to shop. Before malls came there was on the seventh floor a fixy restaurant with a limited fare and female-sized portions but there were white table cloths and a fresh rose in a vase at each table. And so it was again now that the Downtown Renaissance had been proclaimed. With a salad and a dessert it was enough. And there was a style show. One of the models was Fatima. She wore something by Monsieur Annette that was the color of a split plum—split in front where her long tan legs scissored about here and then quickly over there though that wasn't really where she wanted to go either and then they took her out again. Surely it was a dress that only a model could wear and then only when modeling. She may have caught his eye on one of her entrechat and she may not have.

Several of the women moved out from behind pedestals on which were placed assorted ceramic cats. One of the cats was Sherry's Buster-fer. No litter box. The Egyptian one wasn't there.

A voice he had thought was someone rude at a table behind him he now recognized as a partially hidden announcer who exulted that now Fatima (everyone's favorite Capricorn!) was coming back in something inspired by the Christian Copts of her native Egypt. Just the thing for those galas at Christmas!

She had on a gathering that looked like layered black veils that one-by-one were see-through though collectively not quite. Around her waist on a silver chain joined by one flowing from her neck was an ornate silver cross that rode pulsatingly on her mons as she went through her paces. After that Monsieur limped to the fore and received the applause of all.

So he called and yes she would go to a gallery opening where the works by the best painter shown were so flat of color they looked more like acrylics than the oils they were. All of them had titles that had AIDS in them: for the most part the pictures were angry that there was such a phenomenon. Fatima was non-committal on their value but he thought the price reasonable and narrowed his choices to three and then to one of clearly defined pink and blue patches over lavender and Easter yellow.

He handed over the cheque to the manager who was a trim and svelte forty then watched her take a red star off a sheet of waxed paper and affix it to the corner of now-his painting. Fatima took his arm and walked over with him to supervise the act. Something passed between the women—a something he had seen before but had never been able to analyze. He knew though that Fatima had claimed him and a new rela-tionship was theirs.

He got to shake hands with the painter who was a clean hulk of a fellow who was smiling and pleasant. Fatima exchanged a look with him too and applied even more of her tourniquet. When they left she said she preferred to go straight home. She was pleased he was willing to spend money.

A life in the marketplace has given me some to spend. If the world is too much with me late and soon and I am involved overmuch in laying waste my powers with getting and spending well at least I can try to spend it on something that will outlast me.

And who would receive what outlasted him?

His children he supposed. She nodded.

She showed him to the front bathroom. Its location he of course well knew though he had not before seen it done in black with a gold ceiling. She as quickly went to her bedroom and her own bath returning with a caftan for him in brown with fine blue stripes. In the interval he inhaled the musk of the room—she must have scented it somehow—and found it took him back to a much earlier fragrance. It was an old scent he decided then recalled it was similar to one his father's third wife wore. Immediately following he realized it wasn't perfume at all but urine. Why had he confused it with Tabu? Fatima handed him the caftan and caught the flavor too and quickly flushed the toiled turned and left. Already she was barefoot.

He arranged his clothes as neatly as he could then washed and dried here and there and put on the caftan. The hair was mostly off his legs up to the sock tops and some was gone from the sides of his thighs. It was possible that he'd lost pubicly too but with no relevant photographs of him as a young man who could know? He lifted the robe in front and put on his wee-wee folded horn-rimmed glasses from a side table where Fatima kept her tooth paste and birth control pills. With dark curly hair in back of him the fellow seemed in the mirror to look a lot like Henry Kissinger. From the side as well as in front. Vell vot do you tink uf de Mittel Easdern tsituation hum?

Henry did not answer but only stared contemptuously. O vell. He replaced the glasses.

The bathroom musk was gone and not missed. Pipes smelled lightly excretory too and cigars did so entirely too much. Harsh toilet training led men to smoke them a Psych professor had told a class he was in long ago. He had asked if women were never harshly toiled trained but was given only a smile for an answer. He had begun smoking a pipe in college to kill time and kept it up after a girlfriend admired it. He didn't stop till he was thirty.

He rinsed his mouth as best he could and went to find Fatima. There was perfume aplenty when he did and incense in clouds under which she lay enfilmed on oriental rugs. When in a leisured moment an hour or so later she lay beside but with her back to him he turned up a corner to check the knotting and found it to be tight and of good if not great quality. There was also a price tag: three times at the least what he could get one for on one of his trips.

And a month later Hassim had just the thing for him. It was a nice Sarouk that eventually declined in price to 2200 ringgit or 800 real money. Fatima's store would get four times that for something similar. He was also shown how it could be folded into a square a couple of feet across and six inches deep and thus fitted into his bag for easy carriage through customs. He left it folded and at the Hilton put it in the bottom of his carry-on which the Indian maid easily hefted into a corner of the closet. Her bindi dot between her brows was black not red: unmarried. He wondered if she read Tarot.

She had never heard of it but did know a very good fortune teller who regrettably spoke only Tamil although of course she could translate for him if he wanted it. He did and she would be off work in a few hours and possibly could arrange it. The cost she was sure would be ten ringgit. He figured cab fare and a gratuity for her would put it as ten dollars American: okay. He noticed also that her right eye was swollen and the flesh around it darker than its opposite.

Her brother did that she said in the cab and he had no right to since he was her younger brother.

Would it be acceptable from an older brother?

O yes of course.

He would have to tell Fatima.

The man who took his palm wore an ordinary sport shirt and cotton trousers and said Clive was married and had two children one of each sex and would have two more children and that he was rich and would get richer could expect to live to be an old man before dying in South America. He would enter politics briefly.

He asked the maid to inquire whether his long-standing ambition to go on stage would be realized: theatre was in a category with politics and South America since he had never considered any of them. The man found it possibly but only if devoutly wished.

Could his fortune be changed? The maid looked at him stupidly: Why of course.

Ask him he insisted so she did. The man was not as surprised as the maid: yes of course he could. He was also advised to avoid Chinese businessmen. A word was used which the maid had trouble translating but finally it came out as something like sharks. Chinese were sharks. Okay.

That night after he turned the lights out and lay thinking of sharks he located a cicak that had placed itself on the ceiling and over toward the far wall. It was holding still and he thought it unlikely to fall on him though he would not want the seven years of bad luck that a chee-chak that graced your head was sure to bring. He would have to beware the Chinese: a warning.

They were the Jews of the Orient: a long cultural history and if no single book in which God was revealed there was nonetheless a general Confucian tradition and a high valuation on scholarship and on industry and on work (especially in one chosen field no matter what field it was) and on family and of course with a set of values like that one tended to rise. And then to be despised. They were the entrepreneurs and they were the academics and they were the professionals and they were the communists: wherever the action was.

He thought again of the cicak: highly unusual for one to be in the Hilton since even if they were not exterminated there were no mosquitoes for them to eat or other bugs so they would starve. Then he looked again and saw in the vague shadow it was not a gecko at all but a small arrow pointing to which way was Mecca.

The paper delivered free the next morning was not the The International Herald-Tribune he had requested but rather The Malay Mail which informed him that according to the PM the USA was trying to foment labor unrest in the country even as it had done in South Korea. Specifics were lacking. And there was an advertisement for hair weaving which he tore out. He recalled that Architects were said to cover their mistakes with Ivy and MDs with Grass and God with Hair. He could not recall where he had seen it. If asked he would have said Ecclesiastes.

After lunch the lumbermen presented a contract that wasn't adequate but they suggested that the Japanese might find it acceptable if he didn't and the Japanese were closer. He pointed out that South America was closer to him and it too had wood. They smiled when he also mentioned Indonesia since there were fewer Chinese left there after the Sukarno fiasco hence businesses were not quite so well run: indeed many workers in Malaysia were Indonesian illegals. They would meet again.

At the weavers he agreed moderately quickly to a job they began on at once since they just happened to have a match for him. By late afternoon he had a part on his left side that showed scalp and rendered the work realistic. It was in a shade he hadn't seen on his head in twenty years but he was assured it was all similar cosmetically to false teeth which of course he would wear if he needed them. Of course.

These workers too were Chinese. The owner said his oldest son had got 80 on qualifying exams and thus was at university. The youngest son would try again but was learning the trade just in case: Indians needed only 70 to enter and Bumiputra 35 but Chinese had to do 80 or better.

At dinner in an Italian restaurant that was part of an Australian chain he decided no one watched his head. Then he took in an Indian film with violence and dancing before he looked for a cab back to PJ when a voice called. It was an extremely pretty Malay who swayed pleasantly toward him: her eyes began at his top and went down to midway or a little below and smiled again. Her face was flat with little arch to the nose but her eyes were round and liquid. Was she perhaps part Chinese No: all Malay. Her name?

Nasi Mee Ayam she said three times before he caught it. He would like a walk And (a flutter of eyelids) a talk?

He didn't care for that no thanks.

Where was his hotel? In PJ. Could she catch a ride with him? He guessed so. Immediately she hailed one that seemed to have been waiting her bidding. The driver was Malay but wore no prayer cap.

In the cab she tried to start to work immediately but was told no. When he moved her hands he noticed an oddity: the Index finger was shorter than the Ring finger which was unusual in women. At least among Anglos. Then he looked for and found a good deal of Adam's apple and let him out with M$10. The cabman noticed nothing but delivered him to the Hilton.

The lumbermen laughed about it the next day and offered nearly the same contract for him to examine and with a small personal package. The money inside was American.

Fatima was absent on his return as he had expected once he opened the door and saw only cushions and hanging lamps with an elephant god where the cats had been. The elephant god he knew to be the god of bachelors and one of the easiest-going of all the Hindu deities. From the kitchen there came with the flavor of curry a lilting voice that invited him to make himself comfortable. He said he would but needed the bathroom first. Incense was burning there on the stand by the sink where she kept her glasses. The toilet was Western and not a squat-on: had to draw the line somewhere. Her spare glasses were still in the same style. When he tried to see through them he discovered that she must have almost no worthwhile vision beyond ten feet or so. The pill container wasn't there. It was in a drawer and far back.

He came out to a—by Indian standards—fair-skinned woman in a gold and silver sari and wearing a long black plaited fall who said her name was Kali.

Mine's Raffles he said Stamford Raffles.

Her mouth dropped slightly before she recovered her Brahmin grace and swaying led him to a cushion. She said she hoped he liked vegetarian dishes. He noticed that her bindi was red.

Necktie

For Christmas Merlyn got a tie from Myra. It was a nice enough one that he could compliment her on it and say how rare it was that a woman could buy for a man: All women think they can and almost none truly can he said. He knew perfectly well that he could not buy for a woman and got her perfume since it was a safe bet if you bought something costly enough. Except with his ex: Phyl had never kept anything he bought her to include the most expensive of scents.

Myra seemed genuinely to like her Opium and said it went with her dark brown hair. He had no idea what that meant but he studied her part as she helped him out of his red challis: she was small though not delicate and the groove was clear as she worked his collar. It was about as perfect as a canal made by the Corps of Engineers—nearly straight but with a jog here and there. A problem of nature or right-of-way must have caused those for the Engineers but he didn't know why Myra did it. Of course she couldn't see the top of her head. There were no white hairs among the brown which she wore thick and feathered at the sides and back. He had plenty of white ones.

She had his old one off and looped the brown silk over his neck with the fat end on the wrong side. He tried to correct this but she lightly slapped his fingers away. She unbit her tongue long enough to ask Did your sons send you anything?

She knit her brow as she worked and he lightly smoothed her skin. She smiled thanks and almost immediately knit it again. He said he got pictures of his grandchildren.

She nodded and stuck the tip of her tongue out the left corner of her mouth. He bent and sucked it and she laughed and shook him away and kept on tying. She had it hopelessly screwed up: a hall mirror in back of her showed that not only was the wide end on the wrong side but it was tied about one-third as long as the other. He waited for her to give up and noted the tobacco flavor of her tongue and watched her fanny shift the opposite way of her shoulders as she worked and reworked.

Did you get anything?

Um Oh. She got grandchildren pictures from one daughter but the other hadn't any children and gave her a ceramic animal for her circus menagerie. He knew she liked elephants and especially if their trunks were turned up. That was supposed to be good luck. He couldn't see that she'd had much of it with two divorces and having to raise and support two daughters on her own in her teens and without much education. And the daughters were mildly estranged at that. Of course it was his daughters-in-law who'd sent the photographs not his sons. But they always got along his sons and he.

Myra set herself back on her heels and sighed. She hooked her fingers inside his belt and said You do it: I give up.

Thought you knew how to do that sort of thing. She had told him she learned how when she began work in a mortuary but then she hedged it by saying mainly they used clip-ons or else one of the men tied it on himself and then cut it in two in back and pinned it on. That was what they did when the widow or children or parents brought the clothes. When on occasion it was a young man killed in a motorcycle accident or some such often there wasn't a tie in the wardrobe. Always a clip-on when they could: easier with stiff necks. She told him he was too tall and tried to rock him a little by tugging at his belt and rocked herself against him instead. He held her there with one hand and got the loop over his head with the other: Perhaps if I were to lie down?

He lifted and kissed her gently. Because of her teeth. She never had admitted to false ones. She worked her arms around him and he waltzed her into the bedroom.

Her apartment was exactly the same as his though backwards since it was across the hall and a lot neater because she kept it so. Her bed was made which was something that happened to his once a week when the maid came but he kept the sink clear and never peed in it when Myra was around.

She often had told him to be quiet because it was only an eight-plex and if she had heard the woman over her then of course she could be heard too. He wondered if she had been overheard in times past though it mattered little: they were comfortable with each other and no one missed a slice from the middle. She had told him that while mentioning that she had cheated on her first husband. She was drunk when she said it and denied it later.

When he tried to press for intimacy she began to turn her head from side to side and then pulled a pillow over it which ended his brief attempt. Something wasn't right. She was breathing heavily and slowly and he asked why.

She shook her head and bit a knuckle. With closed eyes she said Don't ever talk that way don't ever talk that way. She didn't want to think of him dead. He said it didn't matter that he would go to a different funeral home: it was the one that better families chose if they were Protestant. Catholics went elsewhere and anyway hers was across the river. Across-the-river-towns were always manqué. Her shop was across the river.

Just don't.

He went to the bathroom and washed his face. She had clean towels. Always clean towels. The one time they had the obligatory bath together she had put the towels immediately into the hamper. She said she did a load daily so they wouldn't have time to mildew. His ex never bothered with such: he did the laundry.

Then he went back to her and picked up the tie he had discarded when he had thought he would have his way with her. He made a simple four-in-hand knot and noticed it hung nicely but was polyester and not silk. Walter was still outside his trousers so he tied it on him. Walter was his middle name so that was what he called that part of him. Did

157

she like it that way?

She turned over to her stomach and hid her face in the pillows. He couldn't tell whether she was crying or laughing. It was laughter. She turned over to look then turned away. He offered to show her how to tie a knot but conceded that Walter wasn't up to it.

Another time perhaps she said and sat up. She slid the tie off Walter and asked if he truly liked it. Yes he lied since he didn't like polyester. Then he turned it over and saw instructions to wear it with a green or tan or brown suit. He said he had never seen a green suit he would wear. He put on his glasses to make sure of the label. She didn't need such to see and read it and said that was so was it not? He said he resented being told and realized immediately his mistake.

She hung her head and said she was sorry. He tried to pull her up and sniff at her part where a peninsula occurred on the right bank. She pushed him away and said she never should have tried to buy anything for him: she hadn't the taste the money the knowhow to do it properly.

It was useless to protest but he did so anyway: Look it was my only present. Beside the photos.

She pushed him away: Were the photos all right?

The tie is all right: I love it because it's from you.

Did your wife did Phyl buy you ties that were all right?

She never bought me anything. This is us. Did your exes buy you perfume?

Not as good as yours.

Huh? No she said they didn't buy perfume as good as he bought. Oh. Then she pulled up and rested her head under his chin. Did he want to go out or should she fix them something there? They could read in bed and eat off trays. Or did he want to go out?

Are you on call?

Only for emergencies: the same as for you.

He would not be called by the paper short of a tornado passing through. He said he thought they should go out though already she had a bathrobe out. It was not rumpsprung: he never had seen her in a rumpsprung bathrobe. She said okay and refolded the robe. She told him to wait in the living room while she got ready and he looked for his new tie but couldn't locate it so her put on the old one.

The restaurant was in a till-recently declining neighborhood that now had a rejuvenated movie house and a bookstore besides several new restaurants: theirs did crêpes and specialty soups and had paintings by local artists. She disliked the art and he thought he did too. One looked like a Georges Braque but that was wrong by decades.

She once found the onion soup too chewy but liked the club sandwiches and had one while the men next to them were discussing an old film: one said Salieri wouldn't believe Mozart was better and the other said Salieri wouldn't know Mozart was better. Merlyn whispered Same thing to Myra. Which was when her pager rang: did she want him to be dropped off at the apartment or did he want to go along? He would go. Then he paid the bill and she left the tip. It was too much of one: once he had said she left not enough and ever since she had overdone it. He could feel his face burning.

It was an accident in which a couple had been killed and her Home got them both. She would do the woman. It was an advertising point that they had a female director.

It's not a mess she said Or Church would have said. We'll have to get you out by daybreak but the paperwork's done so no one will be there but Church.

The info already was in to the paper: people liked to see their names in print even if bereaved. As they motored along he put C and W on the radio and Myra began to shift her butt back and forth to Cash's All Over Again. C and W was a point they had in common.

They drove on through a genuinely declining region then over the bridge and past renewal projects and then the former brick merchant's mansion that was now the Home where the trees lining the rain-silvered sidewalks grasped like the hands of naked grotesque supplicants long-buried. When they parked he got a soft kiss and then they went in. The pair of them were naked on slabs with their heads posed slightly to the right. A smiling voice behind them said Don't touch!

Hi Church: this is Merlyn. He's going to watch me do my stuff.

Church excused himself to wash up and Myra circled the woman even as she took off her coat. Then she put on a long lab coat and latex gloves. Church came back wiping his hands and said So you're the famous writer.

Writing that's dead before the ink is dry.

Church reads your column: he knows forte adverb from forte noun because of you.

Church had his jacket on and was smiling his way out: his lapel had a scimitar in it. Notice the bow I tied he said pointing at the penis: Some of us got it and some don't! He pointed a finger at Myra and telling her to look out for the second set of teeth he left. Myra pointed a finger at him too but an upraised one. Church had on a brown polyester tie.

Second set?

A joke she said About a naïve boy who believed his mother when she told him women had a second set down there and would bite him. When a girlfriend showed him otherwise he said he wasn't surprised considering the shape her gums were in.

He said he'd never known a man to fear such.

She shrugged and kept busy washing and spraying and stuffing orifices: at least she hadn't any bows to tie. A device like a boxer's mouthpiece was put between the woman's jaws. Then she emptied and filled cavities and did her hair and nails and was ready to go. A few windows in nearby set-too-close-to-the-street houses were yellowed but not many. Did she want breakfast? No. She laid her head back and immediately went to sleep.

When they got in he offered to cook breakfast but was turned down. He asked about the tie. She had given it to Church.

I would have worn it.

It's a matter of style: our apartments would cost less somewhere else. I know you have to pay for style. She paused and asked if Phyl had style. She put on a fresh and also unrumpsprung robe.

Yes. He'd gotten her at Northwestern: classy school which certainly did not represent the casserole life. In her generation he said The students dressed like nouveaux pauvres. They looked to reforming the world.

Phyl also Plan to re-do the world?

No: only me. Then she gave up on that and after much thought reinvented herself. In a way that did not include me.

She's pretty she said I've seen her. Myra paused and asked if Phyl was a virgin at marriage.

And for two weeks thereafter.

She choked on her coffee: Walks she said Like she's afraid her cunt will fall out.

He hadn't heard her talk that way before but it was dead-on. When she apologized he waved it off. But he asked about Church.

Once she said Long ago: you got to kiss a lot of frogs first. You she assured him Are most definitely and at last my prince.

He laughed and said the trope was sexual in that all men had a little frog—a pink or tan or brown or black frog (depending on the color of the rest of him)—which if kissed by a princess would turn into a tall and handsome prince.

She laughed at that and then reflected: I'll bet Phyl never....

No he said. Then he looked at her knicknack shelf and asked which figurine was new from that Christmas.

She turned and ran water to wash the cups. She was doing so more furiously than they could possibly need. None of them she said: Peg was killed in a crash five years ago. Burned. And my sister sent the pictures: she raised Sue. She raised Peg too.

Then she shuddered and wept. And wept. When the worst of the convulsions were past she moistly said Bed then wiped her nose.

When settled he tried to hold her in a way that when they awoke would have insured a case of Bridegroom's Shoulder for him had she allowed it but she turned away: Promise not to look!

Since she had left the light on he closed his eyes but he heard her do something that sounded vaguely mechanical. Then she went under the covers and in a short time Walter began to think princely thoughts. But it was odd.

Oh my God her teeth were out.

He wanted to tell her she needn't and then tried feebly to stop her but she kept on. Finally he put the pillow over his face to hide his eyes from her should she surface but he began to choke and could not stop and then could not quieten the sobs.

Don't laugh she slurred Don't laugh.

He tried to tell her he wasn't laughing but couldn't manage the words.

Pietá

Leila got the idea that she could tell fortunes when her friend Alec—not quite yet her friend—seated before her in the lounge of his fraternity house took her hands in his and moved them in parallel on his primly parallel thighs saying she had the eerily long fingers of the mystic. Leila thought she could predict fairly well why he had put her hands where he had and she told him so.

Alec smiled with his eyes and said only Oh you cool blondes you Scandinavians you Swedes. He had dark brown hair though looking again at it she saw suddenly that he dyed it so. Probably from blond also. Norwegian she said. She stood up but he took her hands again and held on. He was of average height and had he stood would have been nearly as tall she. He said he wanted to be her friend.

She doubted that but then it came to her that he could be. Collapsing she sat back down. She too wanted a friend she said of the opposite sex. Then she put her hands on his thighs and pressed: But you're in a fraternity—I mean well are there others? Her brother was a member or she wouldn't be there. He shook his head: Maybe there are a couple of them who don't yet realize it. But it's best not to say or do anything that would reveal one's hand.

Isn't it torture for you?

He said that was why he needed a friend.

And so they became friends and Alec who showed her his also tapered fingers began to teach her palmistry. Also Tarot he said But it's more for short-term use: the hands have everything there in general detail. He assured her that Tarot was a necessary adjunct since one

163

couldn't have one's palm read every month the way one could cards: hands simply didn't change that quickly.

Change? You mean it's not fixed He shook his head and allowed that almost anything or anyone could change but few wanted to. He saw she was asking Did he want to? and he sighed and said he didn't know: perhaps when they got to be better friends. She smiled and said okay.

So now he had a date for the parties held at the house every other weekend and she had somewhere to go and could turn down other guys. Not that she encouraged them to ask though some she found to be cute. The only awkward part came when enough beer had been drunk and the same songs had been sung a number of times and the dancers thinned out. Though they both could have danced all night they had to quit then too and they too had to go somewhere to make out.

Neither one knew really how to do it. So they developed a routine where he would lightly kiss her cheeks and then they would hold each other cozily and nuzzle. She told him he could pretend it was someone else if the wanted and he said he was already doing that. Was she? She said she didn't think so. He said he was flattered but drew back slightly and brushed her breast.

Your figure is girlish he said. She told him he didn't know the half of it and looked about in the half dark and put his hand inside her blouse and under her brassiere. He was flustered but took the other side too.

Maybe more like boyish she whispered. That was all right with him of course.

When spring finally came or almost came Alec's fraternity rented as usual a lodge for three days and held their Spring Weekend Party there: it was a good time for them and a chance for the lodge owners to try out their facilities a week before the season officially began. They rode up with Leila's brother Anders and his girlfriend and were the first to get there. Sherry and Anders likely would marry though not when he graduated in a few weeks but maybe a few weeks after that. Sherry put her right hand back for Leila who asked for the left one too which she offered to Alec.

164

One marriage she said. She looked more intently and said Soon. Sherry smiled at Anders and nudged his foot pedal leg with her socked foot which made them speed up momentarily. Alec agreed: Three children he said. Then Leila said In July: you will marry in July. Sherry wondered where that was in her palm.

It wasn't there at all of course but Alec quickly pointed a ridge under her smallest finger: There it is. Sherry drew her hand back and held it in the other while smiling fondly on it as if it were her firstborn and already cuddled by her. Then she turned back and smiled at Anders for many miles though he only kept his red-haired head fixed straight forward. Already there was a dime-sized bald spot on the crown. Or maybe it was a scar.

Alec looked from cornered eyes at her and with his right hand indicated a swelling of his stomach. Leila took his left and thus they rode on to the lodge. Once there she asked if it were a certainty.

Well! You're the one who saw the marriage.

She allowed how that was so but said it was only seen and not in the palm. He said he knew that. She asked But is she pregnant now I mean is there some rational way that I can tell she's already pregnant— maybe she smells some way or other—only I just don't know it? Rational in principle I mean?

Alec said he didn't think she was yet pregnant: Ask again on the way back.

Maybe she should warn Anders? If it—whatever it was—was preventable?

Go ahead Alec said And see what good it will do.

So after dinner just as Alec was getting ready to play the piano for them all—his usual role—and Buckley Campbell was telling those gathered there how much they appreciated Alec's last performance with none forgetting his sensitive rendition of everyone's sentimental favorite I Love You So Much I Could Shit she took time to tell her brother to be careful. This she had to shout over Campbell's being himself shouted down as soon as she said the expletive. Unless he wanted a July marriage he should be careful. Already Anders had four beers in him or five and nodded absently. Maybe she should have told him earlier though the beers also were his choice. Really she couldn't imagine pregnancy. Meanwhile Alec was playing I'll Be Seeing You.

Each cabin had two bedrooms with two people in each so she and Alec stayed out long enough on the beach that Anders and Sherry would already be there and have the door locked. They held hands and walked and threw stones until it was late enough for Sherry to leave and for Alec to go in. He saw her in to her cabin and used her bathroom and came out disgusted. She asked if Sherry had neglected to flush the toilet or worse wondered if she herself had forgotten.

No he said It's just this thing I have about soap with hair on it. She looked in and saw the bar of Lux did indeed have short brown ones engraved here and there: Not mine she said. He nodded then kissed her cheek and left. Just after Leila got into her own bed Sherry came in with the careful dignity of the drunk then sloppily got into own her bed in the dark. Soon she began to make noises of discomfiture before turning quickly to the edge of the bed and vomiting voluminously. Sherry had turned away from the aisle between the bunks though and she puddled most of it on the far side of her own bed. Then she rolled toward Leila and began to snore. With the windows opened a little more the smell dissipated sufficiently that she could herself get to sleep and did so.

The next morning she met Alec at the dock where they took a canoe and began to paddle out around the coves. He had doughnuts and milk for them. It was cold but after a few minutes of paddling they took off their jackets. They found a patch of sand that had taken such morning sun as there was and was one that had a small and clear pool hidden behind it. Alec thought it might just be warm enough for swimming at least for the Norwegians among them. She laughed at that and smiled greedily at him and they without a word went back over the ridge separating them from the shore of the lake and hauled the canoe more securely out of sight.

They undressed back to back and then as on cue turned and examined each the other though still with their fingertips out of range but both pointing at the other's seat of consciousness and exclaiming.

She was amazed at his size—totally out of proportion and rivaling or surpassing Anders who was 6'4" and whom she had sometimes espied while he wide-eyed said she had no hair at all. He inhaled deeply and asked if she shaved.

Never.

He nodded gravely and with extended hands they found each other and then waded carefully into the water. They stopped at the knees then went on to the fork and winced and went in chest high. They turned and faced each other and then looked down. She observed that he was peeing. He said So are you.

And so she was.

Hard to do in this cold said Alec But now that we have spawned shall we get out? She said they should.

At first it was warmer out than in and they enjoyed the sun but then there wasn't enough of it and the wind began to chill. As soon as they were dry they started to get their clothes back on. Then he suggested they trade and they did and found everything fit approximately. They lay side by side on their blanket without touching.

I've never been so clean in my life he said. She agreed: everything was clean—the water, the sky, the trees—everything rinsed and wrung and then dried by Fall and frozen clean through the Winter and now just emerging. She said it was like Easter.

On that note said Alec while studying the cloudless sky Do you think yourself an instance of parthenogenesis? He was in pre-med and knew about those things while she didn't and he had to explain that such was at least theoretically possible for Higher Primates. Though of course Virgin Birth was not. He smiled. She said her mother was married and that Leila was sure her own had been no Immaculate Conception.

Were you there then? Anyway that has to do with the passing on of sin—refers to the conception of Mary and not of Jesus. And there could be lots of virgin births so speak that we don't notice because the parents are married and so they don't notice: you'd just be haploid instead of diploid (having only one X instead of an XX chromosome) which would mean you would of course be female (which you are) and sterile (which you certainly are at least for now) and undersized (which you are not). Your height I mean. Well maybe your breasts. But you're tall so I guess it isn't so.

She liked the idea and wanted to play with it: Hey maybe I am and maybe I would just be taller yet say if I had two Xs.

Like say seven feet. He kept his eyes on the heavens.

She flopped her head back down hard: Sure. Why not? Then she turned on one elbow and smiled at him: If all of you had grown to match the middle part of you that's how tall you'd be! He liked that. He said he liked that very much. Except he thought maybe eight feet—the Frankenstein monster's height.

She waited and then told him the truth: she was simply eleven years old and always would be. Or probably: so said her doctor. Most probably. Then she wanted to read his palm. She'd never seen it but when she turned up for inspection his hand that she held he abruptly turned it over: No he said Impossible. Sorry: the teacher is not to be taught.

That the Weekend Party was the usual success was by everyone agreed upon said Alec when the next time there was a fraternity party and he needed a date. He thanked her for making him no longer feeling like a spectator at such. Then he got busy with interviews for med school and was placed on the waiting lists for three. When they saw each other again at Sherry and Anders' wedding early in July (where she was Maid of Honor and he in attendance as a Brother) he told her he was accepted in one a thousand miles distant. Then he went off to speak to others and didn't get back to her. As he never returned to his undergraduate university and she had no occasion to go to New Orleans they didn't see each other again for a long while.

Anders never heard from him either and once he told her that Alec's name was on a list of Missing Addresses sent him by his chapter in their yearly newsletter. That was about the time of the birth of his daughter: Sherry's third child. They named her Leila for his grandmother even as Anders' sister had been named for her. Her aunt took special interest in Leila Three and had her over for weekends when Anders and Sherry wanted time off. Sometimes she had the boys too but usually she avoided it. Her Social Worker job normally did not involve Saturdays or Sundays so it fit. They played card games: Fish at first and then Gin Rummy when Leila Three was old enough. Also her niece was taught how to do Tarot and the rudiments of Palmistry. It would make her popular at college her aunt told her.

Three looked like her aunt except for having red hair and she was comfortable with her aunt. But why hadn't she any children of her own? Because I never married.

Well why didn't you? Why don't you? She threw down her cards and showed everything paired except for an eight and that won it. Her aunt said You're child enough for me.

That took care of it for a couple of years until Three was asking her about boys and about other things having to do with hygiene of which Leila knew little. She referred her to Sherry on the latter and said of the former only that they had baffled her and that she never really had a boy friend or interest in having one.

There was silence for awhile and then Three said with her head bowed over shuffling cards that her mother had told her about a boy Leila had been in love with in college—Alex.

Alec she said: with a c not an x. Yes she guessed so but he had graduated and gone away and never wrote: I last saw him at your mother and father's wedding. Three said a muffled Oh. Her filling breasts rose and subsided: so already Three knew about Lost Loves.

And she became keenly interested in one cute boy after another and enjoyed her new-found power and said how she could make the teachers look at her. But her aunt was no longer the confidante she wanted and the visits stopped. Three had developed fore and aft (midships too) and was a beauty as well as bright. Once after a suggested-by-Leila (Two) Christmas shopping time together at the Mall with lunch paid for by Two at the best place in the Mall it seemed suddenly that Three appeared not to look like her at all but entirely like her mother. Even the hair seemed right. They parted after lunch and

Leila spent the rest of her time in the Mall looking at herself in mirrors as they presented themselves: she was not flat but she was not Three either.

And she kept up her fortune telling though irregularly until she got an early-out pension from her state job and signed on as the permanent social worker at Pleasant View Convalescent Center: one time she set up shop as Madame Arcata at a stall they had at the Christmas Fund-Raiser. Other stalls were for baked goods and handicrafts—macramé and such—but her stall was the most popular. Relatives visiting for the occasion were plentiful but the nurses and aides and orderlies wanted their turn too. Finally she had to assure the last five of them (all orderlies) that she would get around to them the next day: everyone else was either shutting up shop or already had gone. One of them who was the only Straight among them spoke little but Spanish: the other four were paired with each pair interracially.

She saw shortened lines for one white and one black in each pair and told them of impending sickness. They each looked her in the eyes and for each she suggested that they get themselves tested. Both did. Both were positive.

Only the hand of Colombian Hay-soos was a happy one that showed lots of children and much good fortune. The children prospective delighted him. For the others she had to make things up. And then the patients (most of whom were terminal) heard of her. Every time she passed in the hall they called out and sometimes wanted a reading every day or more often. She began to tend more efficiently and thoroughly to her paper work and stayed close by her office.

Then the Administrator asked her to be more available for such things: it cheered them up she said and she knew how neglected most of them were. Also it was harmless.

But it isn't harmless: it's all there. Only most of it is what was and they have very little left of what is to be.

Mrs. Glitz drew herself up to a height that nearly exceeded Leila's and with twice the girth: Then make up something. Something pleasant. Tell them about their past. About their grandchildren and how well they will do. Leila said she had never done so: not in all her years. She reddened when she recalled doing approximately so after the Christmas Bazaar.

Never too late to begin dear.

And so she lied. Only rarely did someone have the wit to curse her if she reported many interesting years lay ahead. One instance was a woman who also had been a social worker: she wondered if any of her efforts had done any good. What was good anyway? She was firm on abortion though and was convinced there should be more of it and free: too many working class people were unable to accept a more reasonable morality. She herself had never married (as was true of many of her case subjects) and was interested to learn neither had Leila. They became friends in the weeks after that until one morning her bed was empty. The man who replaced her seemed to ignore her findings and looked over her shoulder the while she talked. When she finished she turned to see what it was: heavily falling snow.

I used to have to shovel that he said. Hated it at the time. Had to clear a path out of the garage though for the twenty feet to the roadway. He said his children lived in California in a part where it never snowed. He continued to stare out at it as she excused herself and left him.

The people in the end rooms on the second floor tended to be better off and had better pictures hanging: what made a room home was having your family gods to take along. A couple even had oils on their walls: one had a portrait of herself as a young woman and another had a Harvey Joiner. Leila did not know who Harvey Joiner was but admired it anyway. She wondered what she would have to put on the walls when her time came. Her parents and one of herself at graduation. Anders' children as children. None other.

Then she saw one of herself on the wall of a wasted man who appeared much her senior but wasn't. The sparse beard helped age him and she studied his features as he slept to see if he was the young man with her in the photograph. It was indeed Alec in the picture. Taken at the Spring Weekend Party. And it was Alec in bed. Quietly she took down the photograph and slipping off the backing signed it All my love,

Leila and put it back. She would check his paperwork later.

When she came back the next day he was sitting up in bed and looked to have shed a few years. He said nothing when she came in but smiled. His eyes were shining. She sat on the side of the bed and took the hand with no tube in it. He didn't speak until she said it was time to fill in her forms and then he answered as was necessary. And asked had she changed? No she said I never grew hair.

Plenty on top of your head though same as always. His own head was scantily covered and when he sat up with it out of the pillows the beard looked thicker by comparison. She said nothing and he said that he had continued also (like everybody) just as he was. Did he become an MD Yes he said but asked not to be questioned as to which specialty. She guessed what it was and laughed. Had she family? Two nephews and a niece: You remember Anders. Of course he did: IBM wasn't it? It was and he and Sherry were doing well having lately returned from three years abroad. The youngest who was their daughter would finish college soon. ANTH major.

What will she do with that?

She didn't know. Indeed the last paper Three had shown her was about Michelangelo's Pietà and concerned the phenomenon of the Suffering Mother being larger and younger than her Son. Two had seen no significance in it at all and had wondered at the importance but Three seemed to feel she had achieved something remarkable.

They spoke of the times when women got degrees in Education to have Something To Fall Back On in case the marriage didn't work. But of course she hadn't done that. No she hadn't. And had he any family? Anyone? No: died before I did—six months ago. Same disease. Then he turned his hand over and asked to be read.

You know I can't. Not as well as you anyway.

He said he knew that but he also knew a physician was ill-advised to take himself on as a patient. She looked at a palm that beneath the smooth coruscation was much simplified. He smiled and turned it back over.

Why did you come back? To the Twins I mean but more specifically

172

to this place?

He said he had been back—how long?—years. No: decades. Every since residency. I guess we just never crossed paths.

He would not say that he had nearly knocked her into an iced-over gutter one snowy day when he had come out of Dayton's suddenly and hadn't seen her at first. Then he merged into the Christmas-shopping crowd before she could identify him. He would not tell her that.

Yes she guessed their paths had not crossed. But she noted that he had kept her picture.

He nodded and went to sleep.

When on the third day she saw him again it was snowing again although he saw it as if for the first time: he said his friend John used to say that the first snow of the year was like a religious conversion. He stared out the window for a long time.

My friend John he said: He was religious—never got the hang of it myself: John said that when snow happened overnight it was the best since you woke up as from the dead and were amazed the world could be the way it had become and that it had such possibilities and was going on that way all along only you hadn't known it.

Snow like grace is always going on about us save then we see its slow descent in ragged Christograms....

That's from a poem he liked.

She said she liked it too but noted that the snow did always melt eventually. He agreed: And then it is Spring.

She put aside her clipboard that she carried to look official even when she didn't need it and sat beside him on the bed and put her arm around his shoulders. Eventually they both focused on the photo. He said it was an important day for him: it was a turning—especially when they got in the pool.

Her face burned at the thought of her nakedness: not from birth had it been exposed to any until then and never again. She had at first forgotten it and had to be reminded of the pool. We got in it he said Both naked. You don't remember?

He couldn't quite get his face round to her and she didn't make it easier for him to do so.

Honestly she hadn't: naked yes and lying under the cold sun but nothing about a pool. He sighed: Well it was important to me. I don't know why but it was then that I decided finally to go into medicine—I hadn't decided finally until then. Maybe it was even then I decided on Family Practice since that's what I was in. Not what you thought?

He managed to look around and up at her and saw her blush and this time not only by way of the mirror: I also decided that you were the girl for me.

But you never called me after that! She moved far enough away from him to see his face. He averted it. You called me every other weekend she said For the rest of Spring Term and that was it—you came to the wedding where as I recall you broke sharply from me and that was it! Why?

I kept track of you: I've been back here twenty-five years and visited before that. I've followed your career and know of your niece and where you live—all of it. He paused and sighed: Why do you think I chose this place? I could have had other ones or simply private care: as a physician I am well provided for.

She eased him back onto her breast. Firm as ever he said Which is one advantage to your condition: never prone to Cooper's Droop. She said she supposed so and stroked his head. Soon he was asleep.

After that she went every day to his side and held him cradled him. It was thus that he died on the first of the month of the vernal equinox. When she found (later the same day) that she was his heir she was not surprised. Earlier she would have been surprised but not then. Though she did feel manipulated as a puppet might be. A puppet who had thought her movements were her own.

Leila Three was riding north with her a month later to the lake to distribute his ashes as he had wished when she said she thought it was rather the reverse: that she had pulled Alec's strings at least as much as he had hers. At worst you were dancing in tandem. Shadowing each other.

Two thought of that the next day as they paddled the rented canoe toward the cove and their pool. When they got there she had Three wait around the bend while she walked over the hard sand with the canister firmly grasped. She wondered whether she should disrobe for the event. Certainly should she do so she did not want to be seen by Three or anyone else when she was naked.

So Long as You Don't Hurt Anyone Else

It was a brilliant and in every way excellent morning with the air clear and the sun warm on his back without being hot. The temperature was so perfect that there seemed not to be any temperature at all. The surf slapped decently two hundred yards behind him as he passed beneath an arch of sheltering palms that formed a sort of marquee to the POSH. Now what in hell does that mean he asked a man he thought at first to be a doorman and who really was a British Admiral in full dress uniform. Port Out said the dignified officer and Starboard Home —that was the best way to go out East from Britain. And return home of course. He saluted politely with a touch to his feathered hat and with a hand on the hilt of his sword placed the other on the far shoulder of a very young sailor and moved off. No by damn it wasn't an Admiral it was Sir Cedric Hardwick dressed like one. With a sailor boy. He shrugged and went on in the POSH.

It had been gray in New York and he had wanted very badly to get out. Even before completing all the calls a Tech Rep had to make. The plan was that Frances would find a reason that would allow her to get away and they would meet coincidentally. On opening his door she would be there before him on the edge of the bed. When he would look again already she would be down to the buff. And so had it happened but then his brother had come in. Who also was her husband of course. But that was then. They would meet again as soon as she was well.

The front door to the POSH opened automatically and a pretty bell hop came up and insisted on taking his bag. She had on a pink pill box hat that her sort wore and a hot pink suit. It ran from neck to fork with

177

lots of silver buttons up to her elbows and from shoulder to waist in closely planted rows. Red satin high heels lengthened her legs but hardly seemed to help her with luggage carrying. The lobby had lots of chairs in it—leather ones—and a high ceiling with a gold and glass chandelier. He hadn't seen anything like it except in the movies. The people in the chairs looked as if they didn't need to do anything if they didn't want to. There were slowly moving fans placed here and there for circulation. Like in the movies. Of the best sort.

The desk clerk was somewhat oily but polite and seemed to have been expecting him. He wore a white dinner jacket and withdrew discretely to let him sign in. The bell girl stood smiling and just within eye shot.

He couldn't remember his name.

So he made up one. He told the clerk that the Mrs. would be along shortly which the clerk acknowledged with a short nod. Obviously of no interest to the clerk. He spoke decently to the girl and asked her to take Mr. Leamington to his room.

Leamington. What an excellent name: there had been a hotel by that name in the Minneapolis of his youth though he had never had occasion (or money) to stay there. Then when he turned to follow the girl to the elevator he saw that her costume ran in back to just short of her dimples and then cut down to a sort of V between them. She was bare: no stockings. They were alone in the elevator after she closed the doors.

He cleared his throat slightly and she brought the car to a neat stop between floors and smiling at him over her shoulder she switched off the lights. No one rang for service though it seemed an eternity.

When she turned the light back on she was properly arranged and she took him matter-of-factly to his door then showed him about his room. He was still looking at the ocean when she would have left without a tip had he not moved quickly to catch her. He gave her a five and wondered if it should have been more but she refused even that: le service est compris. She smiled and left. Though he had not been looking away from her for long he saw his clothes were properly hung or shelved and his bag put away. Amazing.

He rang room service for a club sandwich and a pricey beer then went to the balcony and looked down on the beach. It was not particularly crowded and the hotels on either side were not too close nor were they quite as new and flashy as his though they were okay. He sat on a padded wrought iron chair and hardly had got his tasseled white size thirteens on the table when room service was there. He yelled for him to come in decided to leave his feet up. They were new shoes and of a synthetic material that would never need polishing.

It was a girl who brought the beer and sandwich not a boy as he had thought usual. Her hair was the color that Petty used to put on Miss October: a red that suggested Fall and turning leaves and crisp weather. Out of black patent leather pumps rose black net stockings ran half way up her thighs: the stockings were held there by lacy 1890s garters with cloth rose buds on them. And a starchy short white apron plus a sort of maid's cap and that old buddy was it. Her lips were red the way girls' were in WW2 which war he had just missed. She set his place next to his feet and asked with her manner if there was something more. He said Sure and she knelt before him while he ate his sandwich and drank his beer with as much savoir-faire as he could manage.

There was no one on any other balcony but he kept looking from time to time anyway. When she finished she tidied him and refused a tip: le service est compris. He thanked her and then noticed a pair of eyes looking out from behind a slightly raised shade in the next apartment. Son of a bitch!

She came back quickly and was just in time to see the shade descend. Oh him she said. Pay no attention: he just likes to watch. He's harmless. She again picked up the tray and prepared to leave.

What do you mean harmless?

Just that she said from the doorway to the hall: He doesn't harm you does he? No he said. Well then she said Why not leave him alone to get his kicks. If he doesn't hurt you. He just likes to watch. No one gets hurt around here. We do what we want to do and no one gets hurt. She closed the door. The shade was again down.

In the shower he felt better about it partly because he just felt better for having a shower. He shaved and put up his razor and had just splashed on some Aqua Velva when he again had the feeling of being covertly stared at. He tensed and fully opened the door he hadn't quite shut and stood there in his towel wrap and terry cloth slippers ready to do battle.

What he saw was a girl who looked something like the Edward Munch painting called Puberty except she was younger even than that. Just as naked. Her clothes lay wadded on the floor beside the bed she sat on while looking distantly off at nothing. He had seen the painting at the Minneapolis Art Museum when he was in his teens: that was when he learned that dirty was okay if it was Art. He would have liked to have been an artist except he had no gift for it. She asked if she could shower and he said for her to do so. He looked at her garments once the water started running and saw they were not clean and were rather small and she wore what must have been the next step up from a training bra.

When she came out she asked if she could sleep there for a while and he said yes. Aware of his own fatigue he got in the other bed and swiftly faded out of consciousness. When he came up enough to be lucid he noticed she was in bed with him and had snuggled up with one arm draped over him and holding on to him where she oughtn't. He woke her and told her not to do that she did not need to do that sort of thing. I know she said And neither do you but here we are. He resisted for a bit and then conceded. When the sky was darkening she got up and put on her clothes. Where was she going? Somewhere else she said When I find an open door.

Were there many open doors he asked and she nodded and went out. He fell back to sleep. He did not like sharing his bed for sleeping.

Morning coffee and rolls were brought by a brunette wearing boots apron and cap. She served him appropriately. The elevator operator was black in a copper toned tunic cut out in front. She stopped the car between floors three and four.

He left his key at the front desk with the clerk and went on through the lobby filled with the same lizards as before. Except it seemed there were more slowly turning fans and there was Peter Lorre hiding partially behind a pillar. But Pete didn't seem particularly interested in him so he went on.

Outside was balmy but balmy like it is before one hell of a big storm. Except there were no clouds and no storm came. It was quiet. Still. People moved about in silence with each on his business though not at all hurried. The arcade he walked along reminded him of something but he couldn't place it. Yes he could: it was like a painting by di Chirico that Frances had on one of her walls. His brother's wife. It was an insane painting with lots of perspective and plenty of shadows but they lacked proportion and came from wrong and conflicting directions. It made him dizzy to look at it. This was a little like it in the clearness of colors but it seemed to match more even than that. It was not hot. It was not anything. Airless. To his right as he walked the sea kept lapping in lapping in and getting a little closer. High tide was coming.

Then a small man raced past him and he saw it was Peter Lorre. The man stopped and stepped behind a balustrade and looked back. Lorre was staring as he always seemed to be doing and when he put back his soiled handkerchief after mopping his forehead he showed a shoulder holster. Soon Pete ran off down the arcade and quickly diminished in size and disappeared as a pin head far up where the four sides of the arcade joined.

He felt weakened and leaned against the wall and saw that on the other side of the plate glass window next to him was a Chinese restaurant. Just the thing.

Inside it was red and gold with usual tasseled lamp covers hiding the bulbs. The tables were small and had clean white covers on them. His waitress wore green brocade on her uniform that came almost but not quite to her thighs. You like Chinese food? He nodded and noticed her legs were long and straight and not bowed as many he had seen in Japan and Korea were. And how long ago was that 1951 or 2. Good she said and set a plate at the place opposite his and sat herself down. She unshod her feet and with them invited him under the cloth without caring who saw. When he was restored to sitting she served him hot tea while fussing at the flop on her plate. Then she brought two fortune cookies out of the front of her tunic. His said Trust Your Heart. She wrinkled her small nose and laughed with him until they were interrupted by a slam as Lorre came out of the men's room and looked about from table to table and quickly chose theirs to crawl under That he was hiding was plain but noises under the cloth made it clear he also was molesting the girl. Her nose wrinkled again: He likes Chinese food too she giggled.

In getting up he knocked over the table but it didn't bother the girl or Lorre. A French policeman who obviously was an agent of the Vichy government came in with automatic drawn. On his kepi and lapels were flaming orb insignia like that of the US Ordnance Corps. He ran past the flic and as he got out the swinging doors he heard shots behind him and saw the flic stagger and heard the girl scream. He ran back to his hotel as through a maze of life-sized dummies: no one cared. Nor did those in the hotel: everyone sat as before and the girl in the hot pink bellhop costume winked at him discretely. The oiled clerk was occupied in something of importance on his desk. The fans turned slowly. Then behind a pillar he saw Lorre looking carefully about. The elevator had no operator so he punched his button and waited for the doors to slide to.

Just as did so his sixth grade teacher who sent him to the Art Museum got on with him: Sister Valentine as she was called. She smiled thanks to him for checking the door for her and readjusted her habit which was the same black and white except for where the beads were was a bunch of posies. He asked about that and she assured them they didn't wear that beady trash there. He used to drop his pencil to look up her legs where she had gathered her skirts above sensible black nunnish shoes. All the boys did it. Rumor had it that she wore nothing under the skirts and some claimed to know it was true but he had never been sure until she sent him to the cloak closet one day and then joined him there. It was true. Snow on the roof she said but plenty of fire in the furnace. She was blued there but he had never seen the rooftop snow under the wimple. She knew what he wanted and she popped off the wimple and he saw she was blued there too. He had learned later that she sent quite a few of her boys to the cloak room. He had hated it then and was afraid the other boys would find out. No doubt she counted on that. So he tried on the elevator to pay her back with rough back-door stuff but she liked that too.

No one gets hurt here she told him when she straightened up.

When he got to his room he saw the twelve year old girl running down the hall away from his direction trying door knobs. She found one open and disappeared from his sight. He checked his room for visitors after locking the door and satisfied there were none went into the bathroom to empty his bladder. Then he rang room service for a bottle of Scotch and went back to the bath to run a tub. He was just in it when a girl in a short kilt brought him some first-rate stuff and put it in glasses with three cubes of ice each then undid her wrap and joined him in the warm water. Between them they drank half the bottle.

Later he was leading her out when he heard a noise behind him. He jerked open the cabinet mirror and saw that it was two-way and there was the next door neighbor's face for a moment till a hatch slid shut and hid him. The girl was laughing. He put on such clothes as were available and went to the elevator. The operator was a Scandinavian in a blue loose knit garment laid over a gold one. It hardly hid her. They stopped between 3 and 4.

On their way again she stopped abruptly at the mezzanine to take on another passenger. It was one who looked like a Prince of Abyssinia and before the Prince could get on he left. The car closed behind him and according to the wand that dozed across a semi-circle above the door it stopped between 3 and 4. He thought he heard noises inside it but he didn't care. In season the wand moved again down to L for Lobby and when he walked to the Mezzanine rail he saw the Prince essay forth. His listening had not hurt the Swede nor the Prince and he felt some understanding for his next door neighbor.

He looked around and learned no one was watching him watch. Okay: it was a tolerant place. Then he saw there was an arcade of shops on three walls of the floor—nice places too with only the best in women's clothes and men's tweeds and pipes and sporting goods. The men's shop had stuff in it that was too good for him really: prices for suits started at twice what he'd ever paid for one and those were the ready-mades. If he had worn duds like that in to call on customers they wouldn't give him or any other Tech Rep the time of day. Flits worked there or snobs or both. They ignored him and he them. In the pipe shop they had the very best of every make but again a salesman was supposed to use cigars or cigarettes if anything and they had nothing less esoteric than English Ovals so he said he guessed not to the clerk and left.

In the women's shops were customers who didn't appeal to him at all looking at stuff that couldn't have interested him less. Except in the Parfumerie where a meticulously tweeded and nicely rounded bottom stuck out on a woman leaning forward to point out something stacked on the wall across from the counter. He went past her and had to slide between her and a woman similarly located on the other side so narrow was the shop.

Those fashionable hole-in-the-wall places were like that. Probably their rent was out of sight. He pretended to find something of interest and slid past her again rubbing her again. Again she accepted his apology with a perfunctory nod and slight turn of the head but also it seemed to him she rubbed back. She was far too nice a middle-aged woman for that (the kind that bought what the best magazines advertized) but it seemed so nonetheless. So he needed to get by once again and she unmistakably rubbed back. Returning he posed in back of her and rubbed more. The sales girl was ignoring them: her skinny silk bloused back was turned and her typewriter key ribs showed through.

Nothing like this had ever happened to him except he had read about someone in a Henry Miller novel doing something like that in a crowded subway. She had turned the zipper of her skirt around to where he could use and use it he did. The woman talked meanwhile to the sales girl with the silk blouse and close-cut straight black hair. Ugly. In front the woman rubbed against the counter. When she made a little gasp the salesgirl turned to look at her and then at him. And then back to her bottles on the shelf. He left without really seeing the woman's face. Until he glanced back through the window and saw it was his aunt the wife of his father's younger brother. Dead ten years. No it was not possible.

He went to the desk to arrange a change of scenery and on the way passed a room that was greatly unquiet with table after table of middle-aged playing bridge. They were eating sandwiches with the crusts cut off and filled with some sort of green soft cheese they seemed to enjoy immensely as they laughed and gossiped. They were dead serious though when they looked at and drew out their cards. At the desk he found the same personage as before. Apparently he worked round the clock.

Say uh he said and cleared his throat so that the clerk looked up. Say uh what is there to do around here he said and when the clerk smiled he added You know: besides in the hotel. The clerk asked was he bored? No not exactly but he didn't know what to do.

Do what you want to do.

He only looked at the clerk who smiled and said of course one never did anything other than what one wanted: Just do it without worrying about it he said.

Well I don't want to hurt anyone else.

You won't said the clerk shuffling some papers You won't: everyone here is doing what he wants.

Really?

Really.

Those people playing cards. Do they ever do anything else?

Seldom said the clerk: They're quite adept at what they do. And unforgiving—some recall misplayed hands from fifty years ago.

He didn't care for cards. But the girls: All those girls.... He waved his hand.

Oh yes. And there is an endless supply. He asked what if he turned one down. You won't said the clerk. I might he said.

Have you yet? He pointed to his desk.

In front of him were travel brochures. He filed through them and asked about the bridge players: did they ever let up? The clerk shook his head without looking up. Never he said For them it's wall-to-wall bridge. There's a large poker room on another ell—mostly men there but a few women. You would want to join them? He said he wouldn't and fingered out a flyer for deep-sea fishing and another suggested skiing. Was it a long way to such snowy hills? No time at all said the clerk: It can be arranged. That was his choice and he spent days surrounded by more white than any hospital had to offer. Mainly he remained by the fire with the bunnies but once there was a liaison on a lift while over a deep chasm. He had suggested to his spanking clean Tyrolean partner that they go over the side to fall in a crush of snow and she only laughed and said it was not forbidden. Actually Verboten was what she said. She pointed to the lift ahead of them where Peter Lorre was looking furtively back at them. No he was looking at what was at their own back.

It was the Vichy policeman. Lorre got off when they did too but was pushed aside by the flic. The girl waved bye-bye as he turned to chase after them on a snow cleared street. They dashed into different doors of a train that closed just before he could get in. He was stopped from trying by a policeman: Bist Sie Juden? What? Are you Chuish he was asked again. Then he saw that the uniform was not dark blue but black and the lapels had two small stylized thunderbolts on them rather like the esses in a rock band's logo. No he said to the SS man Of course not: I'm not anything.

The Totenkopf man smiled in the peculiar upside down way such persons did in World War Two films and said he thought then that he would not want to take that train. Looking again he saw the cars were old and wooden and those inside were starvlings crowded and dirty. No he did not wish to take that train.

He returned as soon as was possible to his digs and in doing so passed a lush field that seemed freshly mowed on which a few men in long robes were being served what looked like sherbets by dark eyed damsels. The men and women were oblivious to anyone around them and frolicked with abandon He shook his head and went in the POSH and asked whether any mail had come in. No said the clerk without looking up: Did you enjoy the skiing? He said he thought maybe he should have chosen the deep-sea fishing and scuba diving.

No reason you can't leave for it immediately.

Really?

Really. The clerk looked up from his work and smiled slyly: Who knows what delightful creatures you might meet at five or six fathoms beside some pink and lavender coral reef?

He could feel the color rising in his cheeks. Whom would he meet?

Oh anyone: maybe someone you already know. Perhaps Frances.

Frances?

Yes of course Frances. Oh excuse me—you asked whether any mail had come for you and I said none had. I was in error and regret it: there is your letter for you.

It was from Frances. She would be out of the hospital momentarily and would join him where he was. Full-busted and plum-bottomed Frances. As he thought of their rejoining he was momentarily asked by the deskman to excuse him for new customers: a Southern white planter was checking in while behind him a Tom was struggling under baggage he toted. They were admitted.

The clerk smiled at him and told him not to be concerned that it suited them both.

Finally he asked the fellow whether people there had Free Will.

As he said it the fans stopped turning and the hum of activity was gone.

Everyone does what he wants to do said the clerk rather tersely. He returned to entering notes in his ledger: That's enough isn't it?

Am I free to leave then?

If you want to. So may anyone.

Has anyone left?

Not while I have been here. He noticed that slowly the fans had begun again to turn.

Is that a long time? The clerk nodded without looking and said Yes: quite a long time.

He asked whether the clerk had even thought of leaving.

No he said Where would I go?

187

Anyway I like what I do and I am good at it—it is orderly and quiet and it suits me: it is what I did in my secular life and so I continue in it. Only more so.

Secular: he said he had heard that Secularism was the Practice of the Absence of G—.

The word choked in his throat and he coughed and coughed until he got past it. He could not then remember what the word was he had been trying to get out. And the fans had indeed stopped. It was a bad moment until he escaped to the elevator. At his floor he helped the operator by undoing the thirteen buttons on her bellbottoms (except the flap was in the back) but left her to tidy up when he got off to go to his room. When he got there he saw Frances waiting for him in the altogether.

Immediately she ran to him and leapt upon him: Forever she said while embracing him madly: Forever Forever Forever.

ICU

Lazarus entered the hospital on the shortest day of the year after experiencing horrendous pain in his left arm. He let it go for a few hours since he wanted to take his last exam at the seminary even though he didn't expect ordination. The last few years before the Navy retired him he'd planned a second career as a cleric but with his last part-time course work behind him he had decided otherwise. The most orthodox of professors believed in no more than a Ground of All Being—May the Ground of All Being Bless You Real Good the seminary wit said out loud in class one day—and if there was no God the Father hardly could there be a God the Son. One professor found in the researches of Dr. Kubler-Ross much to hope for although Lazarus did not: for one thing the brains of the people in question had not stopped working even if their hearts had and thus short circuits could be going on and off and on. And who they saw also varied according to their culture. Whom would he see? He had no family except for his ex-wife who still survived. Perhaps his mother if deceased would recognize him but since she'd given him up without ever looking at him why ever would she claim him in death?

Then a noise interrupted him: a rounded white female rump was bent toward him as the rest of her was busied with something that faced her away. His wife also had been a nurse but her uniforms fore and aft were starched: when this one turned toward and over him and straightened covers and thereby hovered her bosom above his nose (her name tag on one said Goody) they were rounded and covered with a soft fabric. Still white though. His wife's had always been peaked he supposed because of the starch. Goody was wearing something faintly spicy like cinnamon: his wife had smelled of Chanel #5. Starch and Chanel #5.

One of the monitors suctioned to his side had come off when he turned over in his sleep and Goody had come running: a power pack was also taped to his side (along with the plastic wiring from the three monitors) and a short aerial in the ceiling reported on him to a telemeter at the Nurses' Station. He must have been beeping.

He had not thought of himself as the heart attack type and the annual physical the Navy gave him had never suggested such either. He still thought it a mistake although the VA physician did not. In his blood said the MD were enzymes such as damaged muscle threw off. So they had him wired and he slept watched TV and read. No one came to see him.

He knew a few people in the city and had once had an NROTC tour at the University there and had married there and for a time had owned a suburban house. But when his wife divorced him to marry a physician twice her years the house was sold and their friends in choosing between them chose her. He soon was given sea duty anyway. Now he owned a hundred year old three-storey in an effete inner city section populated mainly by intellectuals or aesthetes or both and a few very old gentility: once elegant it had become available to people of middle means without having first gone through horrific decay. It was an island however amongst other good buildings that had suffered just what his island had escaped. In the surrounding area were three chiropractic offices and four antique shops. Here and there it too was "coming back." A couple of freaky but good restaurants had opened. In the summer there was excellent music to be heard live from several windows sometimes at once which gave a Charles Ives effect except that it was as much pleasant as cacophonic. He was contented in that he obtruded on no one and was secure on his pension. Renters paid the mortgage for him.

On the second floor were two men who fought often and on the third was an artist and he supposed her lover. These last went often to a fashionable slum parish some blocks away and he seldom saw them or the men who went to the same place but less often.

Are you comfortable Commander Lazarus? Nurse Goody had finished straightening the sheets after straightening him. Her brown hair was clean and softly curled. About thirty or a little more: just right for him by the French method where you took half your age and added seven.

Except that I'd like to be able to shower.

No she said that's not possible now. Does your arm hurt?

His left arm had hurt terribly for two days and nights but no longer bothered him. It occurred to him after the pain left that he had strained it while lifting a partially filled heavy box and the cargo had shifted to one side. He would not mention that. No he said Not since yesterday. She nodded satisfaction and giving his thin covers a final pat she left him. His wife was older than Goody. His ex-wife. Though younger than he and she wore considerably fewer years than Dr. Conton. When he saw the fellow for the first time the man had been dyeing his hair and he hadn't all that much to dye. But the man was an MD and Marya couldn't resist that: saw him coming. The jerk's first wife got a large settlement to include two houses even though the kids were gone and the fellow got for his share Marya's starchy body. Years ago.

It was his fault he had failed at marriage since he had no experience with it except externally when the orphans went to people's homes for Christmas. That was torture. Nurse Goody came in with a Coke for him. He thanked her: usually work like that was left to aides or someone else they'd dragged in off the street and rudimentarily trained. Coke: at one of the homes he'd gone to he'd seen a magazine spread on the floor before a real log fireplace but he had been afraid to pick it up although it turned out they had put it there on purpose for him to read since that was where and how their little Mark had read. So that was how he read it: on the inside cover it showed a Kris Kringle enjoying a Coke and cookies in just such a house. Then they gave him some socks. They always gave socks because socks were easy to fit. Orphans consequently were very possessive about their socks: other clothes were

191

handed down or traded but not socks.

He drank the Coke and slept awhile. After he awoke it was dark and it was snowing again. An LPN of sixty or so was adjusting the venetians. Nurse sent you in some cookies she said over her shoulder and he saw a small plate of them. Someone leaving gave them to her and she's on a diet.

She doesn't look like she needs a diet.

Oh sometimes you have to be careful just not to gain it. She left and he ate a cookie. Since they would bring in the dinner of jello pudding and mashed squash in an hour or so he let himself slide into sleep. It was comfortable to rest so: knowing that the term of confinement (however mistaken it was) had freed him from further duties and all he had to do was relax. Then the light came on.

He roused himself for dinner and happily felt more relaxed and calm than ever before. There was however no tray. Instead he heard a chuckle and saw something extraordinary: in the chair in the corner sat Kris Kringle eating one of Goody's cookies and drinking what was left of his Coke. Kris raised the glass to him and drained it. He indicated a small gaily wrapped package on the window ledge. For him obviously. But his fingers wouldn't open it. Then to his further amaze the room filled up first with Nurse Goody and another RN who checked his chest for suckers—there he was lying on the bed while they did it though clearly to himself he stood before an amused Kris—then came he supposed by his youth an intern who pounded his chest and then put a needle into his arm. Goody with her rounded rump toward them in the corner the while was bent over and as if practicing on a dummy had fixed her open mouth on his. It was not erotic and he was put off watching.

Then a whole cart load of stuff came in on wheels and a mask was brought out and so on. He didn't care. He wanted only to know Why Kris?

Who else? Kris ate another cookie. Usually it's children I see but more often than you'd think it's an adult. You're by no means the oldest. The children come with me to see the toys: that makes it easier for them you know. And would be so for the parents too if they could think of it that way. He knit his brows. As for you Commander Lazarus (odd name) you're nowhere near the oldest. What an odd name. You're gentile?

Oh yes. That is I suppose so: it was a fundamentalist sort of orphanage and they went in for names like that.

Kris flexed his belt and pushed it down the better to accommodate his large belly. You've had a full life: you didn't hurt anyone and you paid your way. He nodded to confirm it to himself. But seminary wasn't uh he said and faltered It uh wasn't what you expected.

Well I'd reached the place where there was no point in it unless I wanted to meddle and needed an institutional basis for it.

He saw Goody was out of it now and leaning back on a wall and looking shaken. Kris saw her and shook his head: These nurses if they stay on this floor too long think it is their mission to defeat death. Their mission and in fact their responsibility. He slapped his hands roughly on his knees and said he guessed it was time: for him it was a busy night as no doubt the Commander could appreciate.

Busy?

It's Christmas Eve man. See: even you got a present.

He had forgotten the book-sized box done up in a glistening dark green and tied with a slender red cord. Could he take it along?

Kris was amazed. Then he sighed: You may if you can.

He turned to reach for it then hesitated. But you can't said Kris: You can't pick up anything. He had his sack on his shoulder and was leaving. Coming?

Didn't you bring it?

No. He indicated Goody who now stood weeping. He paused: Another time perhaps?

Kris paused: Yes another time. Kris accepted that and nodded and was gone.

With a rush he lay back on the bed and opened his eyes. All the gear had been taken off him. Nurses and doctor stood in panorama around him each holding a just-withdrawn instrument. He could move his head from side to side but they it seemed could do nothing. He pointed to the package: I want my present. A nurse not Goody picked it up and looking at the doctor hesitated until it was okayed. Goody smiled as she wiped her eyes and cheeks and then advanced herself to assist. He could do it himself and their fingers laced while getting the cord off. It was socks.

Socks with green feet and red white and green rings alternating up the ankles. On the outside of each sock toward the top was an angora-whiskered Santa.

I got them at Macy's she said. I could have knit them myself but I didn't know your size or anything and there wasn't time. He smiled and continued to hold her hand as the doctor listened while skating his stethoscope here and there across his chest.

CPSIA information can be obtained at www.ICGtesting.com
Printed in the USA
LVOW042340130912

298624LV00004B/18/P